A Stranger in the Darkness

Faye Price

PublishAmerica
Baltimore

© 2008 by Faye Price.
All rights reserved. No part of this book may be reproduced, stored in a retrieval system or transmitted in any form or by any means without the prior written permission of the publishers, except by a reviewer who may quote brief passages in a review to be printed in a newspaper, magazine or journal.

First printing

All characters in this book are fictitious, and any resemblance to real persons, living or dead, is coincidental.

PublishAmerica has allowed this work to remain exactly as the author intended, verbatim, without editorial input.

ISBN: 1-60703-581-2
PUBLISHED BY PUBLISHAMERICA, LLLP
www.publishamerica.com
Baltimore

Printed in the United States of America

Acknowledgments

This book could not have been written without the support of many people. To my family, I send a big thank you for all the support and encouragement you have provided me. And for the stolen moments of quiet when I could jot down my thoughts. I also owe a great debt of gratitude to my elementary school principal, Mr. Slywchuk, for encouraging my writing and for providing me with extra work to practice my skills.

Prologue

"Good morning, sunshine! Did you have a good sleep last night?" Dean leaned over and gave Heidi a quick peck on the forehead. As his lips brushed her skin, Heidi's eyes fluttered open. She blinked a few times to bring the man leaning over her into better focus.

"Ummm…morning. What time is it?" came Heidi's muffled reply as she buried her head back under the covers.

"It's six o'clock," answered Dean as he sat down on the edge of the bed. He pulled the covers back just enough to see Heidi's tousled hair.

"Ugh! I hate those words!" Heidi buried herself further under the covers trying to block out the light flooding into the room.

"Why don't you stay sleeping this morning?" suggested Dean. He tucked a stray lock of hair behind Heidi's ear. He lightly traced a path along her jaw line with his finger. "You had a pretty late night last night. I heard you working at the computer until two in the morning."

"I think it was three thirty when I finally gave up," Heidi mumbled into the covers.

"Stay sleeping then. I'll go for a quick jog around the park myself. Then I'll come back and make you breakfast in bed."

"Sounds good. Have fun!"

"See ya, hon. I love you." Dean bent down and gave Heidi another quick peck before heading out the door and leaving her in peace.

Heidi listened as Dean jogged down the stairs. There was a moment of silence during which, Heidi imagined, he was lacing up his running shoes. Then she heard the front door open and close. She imagined Dean stretching out in the front yard, the grey sweatsuit he always wore pulled snug across his lean body as he loosened up his muscles. She drifted back to sleep with Dean filling her dreams.

Warm sun streaming through the bedroom window woke Heidi up two hours later. She rolled over, stretched lazily, and glanced at the clock on the bedside table. The green numbers read 8:05. It was still early for a Saturday morning but late by Heidi's standards. Usually she was up and had an hour's run in by now. Thinking of her morning jog made Heidi think of Dean. He should be back by now and have breakfast ready. Heidi listened for sounds coming from the kitchen but heard nothing. The house was eerily silent. A shiver ran done her spine.

Had something happened to Dean? The thought flashed through her mind. Out loud, Heidi said, "This is silly. Dean probably just stopped for a cup of coffee at his favourite coffee shop. He's probably sitting there right now flirting with the waitresses. I'll just surprise him and make him breakfast."

Heidi kicked the covers away and jumped out of bed. She padded over to the adjoining bathroom to take a quick shower. The warm water felt great against her body. She could feel her muscles slowly loosening and the tension leaving them as the water ran in rivulets down her body. After rinsing off the last of the suds, she quickly dried off, pulled her long, red hair into a ponytail, and threw on cut-off jean shorts and a blue tank top. Bounding down the stairs, Heidi headed toward the kitchen.

Halfway to the kitchen, the doorbell rang. Heidi smiled to herself. Dean must have forgotten his keys again. He had a bad habit of leaving them behind. Heidi had put up a key rack beside the front door to help remind him but it did not always seem to work. Dean still walked out of the house without his keys more times than he did with them.

Heidi opened the large cedar door, still chuckling and expecting to see a sheepish Dean standing on the other side. Her laughter died instantly the moment she saw the two uniformed police officers standing on the front steps, hats in hand.

"Good morning, officers. May I help you?" asked Heidi. A vein of cold fear coursed through her, the uneasiness that she had felt when she first woke up returning.

"Good morning. Are you Ms. Murray?" one of the officers asked. He was a tall, middle-aged man with grey hair lightly sprinkled throughout a thick crop of black hair. He was nervously playing with the hat in his hands.

It took Heidi a moment to answer. She had an urge to say no, to pretend that she was someone else. It was never good news whenever the police came to a person's door in the movies. It could not be much different when it happened in real life. But Heidi was never one to shy away from any situation, no matter how bad. She took a deep, calming breath and confirmed her identity. "Yes. Is there something I can help you with?"

"May we come in, ma'am?" the officer asked. He did not want to say what they had come to say in such an open place.

"Um, yeah. Sure. Please." Heidi stepped back to let the officers enter the house. She showed them towards the living room. It was a room Heidi and Dean hardly ever used except for serious discussions. Friends and visitors were always entertained in the family room off the kitchen. The atmosphere was warm and inviting there. Here, in the living room, the antique furniture and heavy drapes spoke of formality and seriousness. There was no lingering over drinks or good company in this room.

Once everyone was settled, Heidi asked, "Can I get anyone anything? Coffee? Water? Iced tea?"

"No thank you, ma'am. We're fine. My name is Officer Jones and this is Officer Neal," introduced the officer. He nodded to the younger man sitting beside him as he made the introductions. He cleared his throat quietly before continuing. "Do you know a Mr. Dean Murray?"

"Yes. He's my husband," Heidi answered. She looked from one officer to the other. She could feel the panic rising up to form a lump in her throat. Her voice came out sounding strangled as she managed to ask, "Is something wrong? He's just out for a morning jog right now but should be back anytime now."

Officer Jones shifted uncomfortably. He glanced quickly over at Officer Neal and then down at the hat in his hands. Finally, he cleared his throat and said, "There is no easy way to tell you this but…there has been an accident. We need you to come to the hospital with us."

Chapter One

The bus began to gear down as it approached the little hamlet nestled among the towering pines. Heidi woke up from a doze when she felt the change in speed. She looked around her, confused by the foreign surroundings. Slowly, as the fuzziness in her mind started to clear, Heidi remembered where she was and where she was headed.

Buildings began to pop up along the road, catching Heidi's attention. She watched out of the tinted window as they flashed by. Most of the buildings looked familiar, but a few of them were new to her eyes. It had been awhile since she had been back here, though. She had to expect a few changes.

The driver came over the loud speaker to announce the little town on his right: Hadey's Cove. The bus rumbled to a stop outside a dusty Esso gas station, it's rusted metal sign welcoming everyone swinging in the slight breeze. Heidi glanced out the window. There was an elderly couple standing by the door, watching people come off the bus. Two young girls jumped down and ran into their waiting arms. Heidi, still sitting on the bus, could hear their squeals of excitement.

What would it be like to have someone again to meet me with open arms, Heidi thought. She had that all once. That and so much more. But it had all been ripped out of her arms for reasons she still could not understand.

Heidi let out a sigh. There was no use waiting any longer. Nothing was going to change. She had come back to start again, to try to find herself. She was not going to find anything hiding on this bus. Heidi collected her purse and the bag stowed under her seat and moved towards the front. With one last deep breath, she stepped out into the world again.

"There you are, Heidi, my girl!" greeted a tattered old man as he hobbled toward Heidi with outstretched arms. He enveloped her in a big bear hug. "For a minute there, I thought I had the wrong bus. You weren't coming off. But now here you are."

"Hello, Grandpa," chuckled Heidi, returning the hug just as enthusiastically. "I didn't expect anyone to come meet me."

"I couldn't let my little angel come home without a welcome wagon! Your mother, on the other hand," Grandpa waved his weathered hand in dismissal, "couldn't give a care whether you arrived or not."

Heidi took in her grandfather's appearance. While she had written to him regularly, she had not seen her grandfather in a few years. Time seemed to be catching up to him. The creases that lined his face had deepened and his cheeks had sunken in until his cheekbones stood out prominently. There was a slight stoop to his broad shoulders that had not been there before. Instead of the confident swagger that Heidi remembered as a young girl, her grandfather shuffled along with slow, cautious steps. A pang of guilt pierced Heidi. It was one more thing to regret about the past few years.

"Oh, Grandpa. You know Mom is busy taking care of the tourists. It's her life." Heidi defended her mother. Her grandfather had never really seen eye-to-eye with his son's wife. For as long as Heidi could remember, they had been picking away at each other. And for just as long, Heidi had been the go-between, defending one side against the other.

Grandpa snorted. "More like running around with the tourists!"

Heidi could see that the conversation was heading nowhere fast. She quickly changed the subject. "How did you come over here? Don't tell me you drove?"

"Of course I did! How else do you think I get around? There's no fancy taxi service around here like in that big city of yours. My truck's parked over there." Grandpa waved in the general direction of the vehicles parked alongside the gas station. He bent down to pick up the bags that the bus driver had just set down beside them. "Let's get your bags and get you home. I'm sure you're tired after that long trip."

Waving her grandfather off, Heidi picked up two black duffel bags from the ground beside her. She shouldered one bag and grabbed the other with her free hand. "It's okay, Grandpa. I can manage my bags. You just lead the way to the truck."

"Is that all you brought?" Grandpa asked as he ushered Heidi over to where he was parked.

"Yes, Grandpa. I was limited to the amount of luggage I could bring with me on the bus. And besides, the moving company should be bringing the rest of my stuff up in a day or two. I won't need much to tie me over until then. Just a few changes of clothes."

"I don't know why you didn't let me move all your stuff home," grumbled Grandpa.

Heidi chuckled at her grandpa's indignation. He was still as fiery as ever even though he would be celebrating his ninetieth birthday in the fall. "Oh, Grandpa! There was just too much stuff for the two of us to move by ourselves. And how would we have got it up here? Your truck would never have been big enough! The moving company was great anyway. They came in and packed everything up for me. I didn't have to worry about a thing."

"But it's so expensive. I could have helped you for free."

"Oh, Grandpa. I wasn't concerned about the money. I was more eager to get up here to see you. If you really want to help, you can help me unpack. That is one job that I am not looking forward to!"

While Heidi and her grandpa were discussing the move, they walked over to Grandpa's truck, loaded themselves in, and headed up the road into the centre of Hadey's

Cove. A comfortable silence settled around them as they moved down the streets lined with houses. Grandpa stayed quiet to give Heidi a chance to check out her old home town. Heidi watched out the window as her new home, and old, unfolded in front of them.

Grandpa looked over at Heidi when he pulled up to the only stop sign in Hadey's Cove. His eyes misted over and a smile tugged at the corners of his mouth. He reached over to cover Heidi's young hand with his old, weathered one. "I'm really glad you came back, Heidi. Things will be all right now."

"Me too, Grandpa. Me too. And I do hope you're right," whispered Heidi as she looked up at the house standing at the end of the street.

Chapter Two

The house stood guard at the end of a quiet street that wound its way towards the lake. It was a grand house, full of character and pride. A wide, rustic veranda skirted the entire building, providing ample room to sit out and enjoy the view of perfectly manicured lawns and gardens and of the lake lapping gently against the shore at the edge of the property. A carved wooden door inlaid with heavy, frosted panes of glass hid the splendour of the interior from the prying world and, at the same time, invited the world to come in.

There were three stories plus a full attic to the house. Dozens upon dozens of windows hinted at the number of rooms that could be found inside the walls. They were of different shapes and sizes, each adding its own little piece of charm to the house.

As Heidi and Grandpa rumbled down the long lane, a brightly coloured sign nestled in a bed of gay flowers greeted them. It welcomed them to Water's Edge Inn, a Home away From Home.

People were moving around the house—in and out of

the front door, among the flowers and shrubs, down towards the lake and white sand beach. Everyone seemed to be moving with some purpose in mind but at a leisurely pace, as if in now real hurry to get there. Heidi watched the people as they drew closer and wondered how she would ever get used to so many people staying in the same house. It had been awhile since the last trip home and even at a visit, all the people coming and going had grated on her nerves. It was like constantly having visitors that would never go away. But she would have to get used to it. There was nothing left in her life now except this. She sighed heavily.

"You okay, Heidi? Anything the matter?" asked Grandpa, a look of concern on his face as he glanced over at his granddaughter.

"I'm okay, Grandpa. Just a little tired from the trip." The last thing that Heidi wanted her grandpa to know was how sad it made her feel to be back here. He would be hurt and would think that he was partly to blame. Her sadness had nothing to do with him, or the house even. Her life had taken a wrong turn somewhere and she could not figure out how to get back on the right path. She had no idea where to even start. She was hoping that the old house held the secret within its walls. She had been happy here as a child. Maybe she could find that happiness again as an adult.

"Well, once we get all your things in the house, you go and have a nice long nap before dinner," Grandpa suggested. He pulled up to the front drive and stopped the truck near the main doors. "Nana's fixing you up something special for dinner and you don't want to miss that now."

"Nana!" Heidi exclaimed excitedly. She perked up at the mention of the name. Nana had been their housekeeper when she was growing up. Heidi had spent more time with Nana than she had with her own parents. She had become the grandma that Heidi had never had. "Is Nana still living here? I thought she moved down to Poplar Point to live with her daughter."

"She did but a couple of years back, she came up for a visit and hasn't left since."

"It's been ages since I last saw her." Heidi was taken back in time for a moment. She stared out the window, lost in memories of her childhood, of helping Nana in the kitchen and yard, of spending hours munching on cookies at the kitchen counter and of talking about her problems with the gentle, old lady. Nana had been the lighthouse in Heidi's sometimes stormy childhood, a bright beacon of safety in the darkness.

"'Bout four years now. Just after the last time you came and visited us."

Heidi looked over at the man sitting beside her. His eyes were filled with lost memories and his shoulders slumped forward slightly. She suddenly felt guilty for staying away for so long. She took Grandpa's hand in hers and whispered, "I'm sorry."

"What are you sorry about? You haven't done anything wrong." Grandpa shook himself out of his stupor. He looked over at Heidi questioningly and gave her hand a gentle squeeze of reassurance.

"I should have come back more. I should have come to see you," Heidi insisted. She had always found some excuse not to come—it was very busy at work, the weather was not good for travel, Dean could not get away. After awhile, her mother had given up asking and Heidi had lost track of the time.

"You had your own life to live with more important things to do then visit a grumpy old man. And I don't blame you for not wanting to come back to see your mother."

As always, Heidi defended her mother against her grandfather, no matter how much she agreed with him or how worn and tired the excuses sounded. Heidi had not understood her mother's actions at the time, but now she was starting to. Everyone dealt with their grief in their own way. "Mom's not that bad, Grandpa. She's just been lonely since Dad's been gone."

"I wouldn't call it lonely the way she carries on with the guests." Grandpa waved his hand as if shooing away a pesky fly. "But let's not ruin such a happy day with arguing over your mother. We should get you in before people start wondering about us sitting out here in this truck!"

"Okay, Grandpa," laughed Heidi. "I guess I can't avoid this any longer."

Heidi opened her door and climbed out of the truck. She looked up at the house, wondering again if she had made the right choice. Should she have come back here or should she have stayed in the city and tried to move on with her life? Both places held so many memories, both good and so terribly bad.

Suddenly the front door flew open and a woman bounded out. She wore a lime green halter-top and cut-off denim shorts that set of her summer tan. Her hair was a mass of copper curls pinned on top of her head. She trotted down the stairs, her arms extended in welcome.

"Heidi, darling! You're here! I didn't expect you so soon. I didn't think you would be here until later tonight." The woman wrapped Heidi in a big hug. She leaned back far enough to blow kisses into the air on each side of Heidi's cheeks with a well-practised European flair.

"Hello, Mom. I left you a message saying that my bus gets into town just after lunch." Heidi pulled slightly away from her mother. After ten years, she was still not used to such an out poring of emotion. Her mother had always been so reserved and distant when Heidi was growing up. The success of her business had sparked a new, more open outlook on life. While it made Heidi happy to see her mother so happy, she sometimes wished that she had received more of that emotion as a child.

"Oh! Well, it doesn't matter now. You are here safe and sound." Heidi's mother stepped back and took a good look at her daughter. "You look worn out, dear. You have been pushing yourself, haven't you? Well. You are home now and can take it easy. You can put your feet up and enjoy the amenities. We have a wonderful new massage therapist in town who will do amazing things to your body. And Candy has added spa services to her salon that are just to die for! We'll have you looking and feeling like a million bucks in no time!"

"I came home to help, Mom. Not to take a holiday," Heidi protested. But she knew that her mother was only half listening. Her mind was already heading off in another direction. Heidi sighed inwardly. Dealing with her mother was going to take all of her energy and more. At least it would help to take her mind off her heartache.

"Hmmm... That's something else we have to work on." Heidi's mom looked away briefly, as if trying to find the right words to break some uncomfortable news. Not finding the answer in the flower garden running along the driveway, she plunged ahead in a rush of air, "While you are here, do you mind calling me Gladys and not Mom? I just think that it would be more professional around the guests."

"I guess. If that's what you want, Mom...er...Gladys." Heidi looked at her mother curiously. She had changed so much since Heidi was a young girl. She seemed to be happier, more free-spirited. Once again, Heidi wondered if she had made the right decision. It could be a long summer with her mother flitting around. All she really wanted was some peace and quiet and a little time to rediscover who she was.

"Don't want any guests thinking you're old, that's all," piped up Grandpa from where he stood beside the truck watching the scene. "Your daughter might run you a bit of competition."

"Oh posh, Grandpa! You can be so silly sometimes." Gladys waved her hand at Grandpa, as if dismissing a child. "Heidi can have all the men she wants. And there are some real nice ones around here right now." Gladys winked at Heidi conspiratorially.

"I am not interested in any man right now, Mother," muttered Heidi.

"Oh dear. It has been long enough now. You can't live your life alone forever. What you need is a nice young man to get you back in the saddle."

"I need no such thing Mother! All I want right now is a little peace and quiet in my own room," Heidi protested vehemently. Her mother had gotten over the grief of losing her husband by embracing people, but Heidi was different. She wanted to be left alone with her memories and her pain. She would heal in her own time and in her own way.

"You're right. We should get you settled in and let you have a rest before dinner. I'm sure that you're tired after that long trip. I have the maid's cottage all ready for you.

I thought you might want a little more privacy and a place of your own." Gladys linked her arm in Heidi's and led her toward the house. An uniformed bellboy came out of the house to help with Heidi's bags and follow them to her room. Grandpa remained by his truck, shaking his head. He sent up a silent plea to his departed wife to watch over Heidi and help take the sadness from her eyes.

The cottage was a short walk from the house, connected by a meandering stone path. It was hidden from sight by a tall stand of pine trees. Moss was beginning to creep into the crevasses between the red bricks, adding a warm, green fuzzy look to the cottage. White shutters and window boxes spilling over with flowers outlined the windows. A slate blue door led to the interior of the cottage.

Heidi looked around her as she stood just inside the door. Everything looked exactly as she last remembered. To her right was the living room. A large brick fireplace took centre stage, flanked by a large sofa on one side and two overstuffed chairs on the other. The sofa was laden with pillows in a multitude of colours and sizes. A braided rug invited visitors to curl up in front of a roaring fire on a stormy night. All that was missing was an old dog stretched out on the rug and thumping his tail in welcome.

To Heidi's left was the kitchen and breakfast nook. It was decorated in old seaside cottage style. Whitewashed cupboards held pale blue ceramic plates, bowls, and glasses. The appliances had been updated since Heidi had last been in the cottage. A stainless steel refrigerator, stove, and microwave sparkled in the warm afternoon sun pouring in through the window.

"Nothing's really changed," breathed Heidi as she took in her new home.

"I had to put in a new fridge last month. The old one finally gave out. That thing just went on and on forever. I thought it would never quit even though it started to make one helluva racket. And it was such a brute to get out of here! Almost had to take a wall out to do it! But Arnie managed to wiggle it out without a scratch on anything," Gladys said. She flopped down on the sofa and kicked her sandals off. She spread her long, bronzed legs out beneath her.

"Arnie?" Heidi raised an eyebrow in her mother's direction as she moved into the living room. She noticed her mother's cheeks colour slightly.

"Oh. Umm..." Gladys averted her gaze, pretending sudden interest in the couch. She rubbed at the material as if trying to remove a spot. "Arnie's the local furniture store manager and the town's general fix-it man. He helped me get rid of the old fridge and pick out a new one. And the stove and microwave. I had to have everything matching for my baby."

"Does Arnie come around a lot?" Heidi asked. Her mother had never mentioned anyone specific before. Heidi wondered if someone had finally caught her mother's eye again.

"He helps me keep this place running if that is what you mean." Gladys pouted slightly. She was not liking her daughter scrutinizing her life. "I have no man around to do any of the fixing, and we both know that I'm not handy with tools, so Arnie helps me out. He's the town's general contractor and handyman." Gladys jumped up from the sofa and slipped into her shoes. All of a sudden, she seemed to be in a hurry to be going. "But I should leave and let you get settled. I am sure that you are tired after your long trip. Dinner's served at seven if you wish to join us."

Heidi watched Gladys scurry out of the cottage. She knew that her questions about Arnie had bothered her mother. Suddenly, she realized that she would not be the only one doing some adjusting.

Chapter Three

The dining room buzzed with voices as Heidi paused just inside the large oak double doors. The panes of stained glass inlaid into the door caught the candlelight and sent rays of colour bouncing off the walls. There were twenty tables scattered about the room. Most were filled with guests enjoying an evening meal and conversation with family and friends.

Heidi looked around the room, trying to locate an empty table. Out of the corner of her eye, she saw her mother waving at her.

"Heidi, Darling! Over here," Gladys called. "Come join us at our table. We have lots of room."

Heidi threaded her way among the other tables to the corner of the room where her mother was seated. Sitting beside her was a handsome stranger. He was wearing a navy blue polo shirt that stretched snugly across his broad shoulders and chest. The top two buttons were undone to reveal a tanned throat and simple gold chain. Wisps of dark curly hair peeked out from the vee made by the shirt. His dark hair had red highlights scattered throughout that caught the candlelight, creating the impression of a halo surrounding his head. The stranger looked up at Heidi as she approached the table. Chocolate brown eyes with flecks of gold swimming in their depths greeted her. She lost herself for a moment in those eyes.

"I didn't expect to see you here for dinner," Gladys greeted Heidi, breaking into her revere. "I thought you would be too busy unpacking and settling in."

"I don't have much stuff with me right now so it didn't take me long," Heidi answered. She shook her head to clear her thoughts. "The movers won't be here with the rest of my stuff for a couple of days."

"Well, please join us then. There's lots of room." Gladys gestured to the empty chair beside the stranger. She motioned for a nearby waitress to bring a plate of food for Heidi. "Oh! Where are my manners? Heidi, this is Jansen Winfield. Jansen, this is Heidi Murray."

"Pleased to meet you, Heidi," Jansen said. His voice was deep and throaty, sending shivers up Heidi's spine. He held out his hand to Heidi. Tentatively, Heidi placed her hand in his. It was quickly engulfed by his much larger hand as he wrapped his fingers around hers. He applied slight, but gentle, pressure against her hand. An electric current rippled up Heidi's arm from the point of contact. It was all she could do not to pull her hand away. She had never felt such intense electricity from touching another person. "Gladys never told me that she had a sister as stunning as herself."

"Oh, Jansen," purred Gladys. "You are just too much."

Her mother's voice broke Heidi from the trance she was in. Dazed, she pulled her hand from Jansen's grasp and cast her mother a disgusted look. She hated watching her mother flirt with every eligible man who came to stay at the inn. She replied, "I just got in this afternoon."

"It sounds like you are moving," Jansen inquired curiously. He stood up to pull Heidi's chair out and help her get settled at the table.

"Sort of." Heidi sat primly in the chair, nodding a silent thank you to Jansen. It was very rare for a man to pull out a chair for a woman nowadays. Heidi was a little flustered by the gesture. She could not remember having it done before, and so, did not know quite how to react or respond. "I'm taking some time off work and moving back here for a while. I'm staying in the old maid's cottage on the other side of the pine trees."

"What do you do, may I ask?" Jansen asked, politely. He turned in his chair so that he could direct his full attention to Heidi.

"I'm a graphic artist," Heidi answered simply. She picked up her fork and poked at the food that the waitress had placed in front of her. She took a small bite of chicken to fill her mouth so that she would not have to say anything else.

Gladys took up the slack in conversation while Heidi nibbled at her dinner. She leaned towards Jansen to explain further. "Heidi works for a big production company in the city. She's taking some time off to rejuvenate herself. Been through a stressful time and needs to find herself again. This is where her roots are so I suggested she come back here and stay awhile."

Heidi shot her mother a seething look. She did not want every stranger knowing about her problems. She did not want their pity. "I don't think Jansen is too interested in my personal life, Gladys. We don't want to bore him with insignificant details," she ground out through clenched teeth.

Jansen shifted uncomfortably in his chair. He could feel the tension crackle between Heidi and Gladys. He cleared his throat and tried to change the subject. "What kind of graphic art do you do?"

"A little of everything but mostly animated commercials," Heidi said.

Jansen tried to pull Heidi out to generate more of a conversation with her. He was used to working with people who did not want to, or could not, talk. He patiently prompted Heidi. "Must be pretty exciting."

Heidi shrugged her shoulders non-committedly. She pushed the food around her plate, trying to pretend that she was interested in what was in front of her. "It can be at times. It can be dull, too, though. Especially drawing the same thing day in and day out."

"Well, I'll leave you two to finish dinner," Gladys said, breaking into Heidi and Jansen's conversation and drawing their attention back to her. "I really must go and check on the front desk and make sure the Richardson party was checked in properly. The new girl just isn't catching on to our system yet. I'll see you both later."

Gladys rose and sauntered away towards the main hallway. Occasionally, she paused to greet guests as she wove her way through the room. Jansen and Heidi watched her go in silence.

Finally, Jansen turned back to Heidi and said, "Interesting woman, that Gladys."

"Yes, interesting indeed," agreed Heidi, a hint of sarcasm edging her voice. She shook her head slightly as she watched Gladys leave the dining room.

"Did you grow up in this house with Gladys?" Jansen asked, breaking into Heidi's thoughts.

"Sort of. Gladys raised me here. She's my mother, though I'm not supposed to mention that out loud." Heidi smiled to herself. Gladys would not be happy that Heidi spilled the beans about their relationship to Jansen but it served her right for trying to throw Heidi at the stranger. Her mother was going to have to learn sooner or later that Heidi was not interested in a relationship. She just was not ready yet. She was not even sure if she would ever be ready.

"Well, it will be our little secret. I promise that I won't tell anyone." Jansen held up two fingers in a mock Boy Scout salute. "Has this house always been an inn?"

"No. It used to be a plain old house until my dad passed away just over fifteen years ago," Heidi explained. She absent-mindedly played with the napkin in front of her. "After he was gone, Gladys turned it into an inn. She said that she was too lonely in the house all by herself. Said that she needed people around her to keep her busy."

Jansen mentally stored the little piece of information that Heidi had just unknowingly handed to him. He was not sure what he would use it for, but thought that it might prove useful sometime down the road. He had a special talent for finding out what appeared to be useless information. "That's understandable. Gladys seems to thrive on attention. I couldn't imagine her spending much time alone."

"No," Heidi agreed, "she has always enjoyed the spotlight."

"Since you grew up here, I bet you know your way around here pretty good."

"Yeah, I guess I still know the place." Heidi shrugged her shoulders. She was not sure where Jansen was headed with this sudden change in subject.

"Can I interest you in a tour of the grounds then?" Jansen asked, quirking an eyebrow. He smiled shyly at Heidi in an attempt to convince her that his intentions were purely innocent. "I have only been here a couple of days but have been itching to do some exploring. I haven't had much of a chance before tonight."

"There are guided tours during the day," Heidi suggested, unconsciously slipping into tourist guide mode. Though she had never worked at the inn herself,

Heidi had felt it important to know all about the place and what it had to offer. She may not have agreed with what her mother had done with the house but she did support her. Heidi did what she could to promote the inn without being too obvious. "There's different lengths and difficulties of hiking trips for all skill levels."

"I know. But I want some more hands on experience. I want to learn the stories behind everything," Jansen pleaded. "I'm a real history nut."

"Well, okay. I guess." Heidi relented. She just could not resist Jansen's puppy dog face. "A walk might do me some good after that long bus ride."

And a walk through my old haunts might help to ease some of the pain and anxiety of being back here, thought Heidi. She had no desire to go back to the cottage right now. Maybe if she walked long enough, she would be exhausted enough to fell asleep right away and the loneliness of the place would not bother her for one night.

"Great! Let's go." Jansen jumped up from the table, tugging Heidi after him. He led the way through the dining room to the front door. He held it open and motioned for Heidi to go through first.

Heidi and Jansen walked among the towering maples and oaks and pines, across carpets of green moss, and through leafy ferns that tickled their legs. Heidi described the history of the area: how the trees were planted; where, as a young child, she had held secret meetings with friends; why certain trees were planted where they were and not somewhere else. They ambled along aimlessly, in no hurry to get anywhere.

Heidi's mind was only half on the trails as she led Jansen through the forest. It kept drifting to the stranger walking behind her. Her heart had stopped for a brief moment when she had seen the man sitting at the table. Then it had started beating double time, so fast at times that it would miss a beat.

It was the same feeling that she had had when she had first seen Dean as he walked into tenth grade chemistry class. It was the same intense chemical reaction, if not even more so. She had thought that she would never have that feeling again. Now, after only a few hours of being back in her childhood home, the feeling had flooded her senses.

It's just a coincidence, Heidi thought to herself. Just old memories resurfacing. It doesn't mean anything. Heidi tried to convince herself but all her arguments seemed to be empty. She could not shake the nagging feeling that something had brought her here. She had been meant to come back home. Heidi tried to push the thoughts away, to clear her head and concentrate on describing the forest around them.

The worn path led Heidi and Jansen to the edge of the forest. The trees opened up to a small, sandy beach and wide expanse of deep blue water. Sea gulls called to each other as they bobbed among the waves. The sun was just starting to sink into the blue depths of the horizon, turning the sky brilliant shades of red and orange and pink. A grey squirrel scurried across the sand and back into the safety of the trees. It cursed loudly at Heidi and Jansen from the safety of the branches for disturbing its play.

"This is the east end of the lake," Heidi explained. "We used to come down here as a family and have picnics and go swimming. It was sort of our own private beach."

"It's beautiful," Jansen whispered, as if afraid to break the peacefulness surrounding them. "And so quiet."

"Guests aren't really allowed down here," Heidi said. She took a deep breath of air, trying to suck in some of the calmness of the spot to soothe her troubled thoughts.

"I feel so honoured then."

"Yeah, well, just don't tell anyone. I still come down here when I come home to visit. Some days it is the only time that I can be alone."

Heidi sat down on a moss-covered log, hugging her knees close. Jansen settled on the log beside her. Their shoulders brushed lightly, igniting sparks in Heidi. She stiffened but could not move away without looking rude. Taking shallow breaths, she tried to hold herself very still to avoid any further contact.

They sat watching a seagull diving deep into the dark water after treasures that only it knew about. Neither Heidi nor Jansen wanted to break the silence. They were content to just sit quietly together, soaking in the nature around them.

Heidi slowly began to relax, her breathing returning to normal and her muscles loosening. She shifted slightly on the log into a more comfortable position. In doing so, she found her thigh pressed against Jansen's. She could feel his heat sear her skin even through two layers of denim. She sucked in a breath. But she could not get her muscles to listen, to move away from the heat. Instead, her leg stayed stubbornly in place.

Heidi peeked over at Jansen from the corner of her eye to see if the contact between their legs was affecting him like it was her, but he seemed to be too caught up in watching the seagull. A half smile curved his mouth upward. Heidi's eyes stumbled over Jansen's lips. They were softly rounded and glistened with moisture. They were the rosy colour of her favourite flower. They beckoned to be kissed. Heidi imagined running her tongue across their silky surface, nipping lightly at the bottom lip. She suddenly wanted to taste Jansen's lips, to see if they tasted as sweet as they looked.

Jansen turned and looked over at Heidi. She coloured slightly at being caught staring. His half smile deepened and his eyes twinkled with laughter. But Jansen did not say anything about Heidi's close scrutiny of him. Instead, he said, "It must be tiring having strangers around all the time, poking their noses into your life."

Heidi tried to clear her head to think of something to say. She was too embarrassed at being caught staring to be able to think of anything clever so she said simply, "I had left home before Gladys had really got the inn going so I have never really had to live with all the people being around all the time."

"But you're back now. You'll have to start living with them now," Jansen countered.

"I guess. But I have my own place so I'll have some privacy I can stay away if I want," Heidi pointed out, shrugging her shoulders. "And living here really won't be much different than living in the city. There's always people coming and going in the city."

"True." Jansen pondered Heidi's logic for a moment. Then he tried to catch Heidi off-guard by suddenly switching gears. "Why did you leave the city? You don't seem to excited to be back here."

"I needed a change of scenery," Heidi said abruptly. She hugged her arms close, as if suddenly chilled. "We had better head back. It's getting late. It'll be dark in the trees now that the sun is setting and we didn't bring a flashlight with us."

Heidi stood and headed back up the path. She did not wait to see if Jansen was following or not. He stood watching her retreating figure and then, sighing quietly, started to follow her back up the path to the house.

Chapter Four

When Heidi had first approached their table, Jansen could almost see the shroud of pain and turmoil surrounding her. Although she had smiled in greeting, the smile had not quite reached her eyes. An overwhelming desire to wrap his arms around her and kiss away the pain had washed over him. At the image of her in his arms, a heavy ball had settled in the pit of his stomach. He could not allow himself to get too close. Too many things could go wrong and jeopardise everything. For a brief moment, as Heidi had settled herself into an empty chair, Jansen had thought that maybe coming up here had been a bad idea.

Jansen shook his head to clear his thoughts. He had had to disappear for while and he had not been able to get the picture of Heidi out of his head. He had to come up and see how she was coping. And besides, he thought to himself, smiling, the perks were undeniable. With a sexy backside like that, he could follow it anywhere. He might not even mind being stuck so far from all the action.

Heidi had stopped at a fork in the path and was

watching as Jansen caught up. "If you keep following the path here," she said as she pointed to her right, "you will get back to the inn."

"Aren't you coming too?" asked Jansen.

"No. I'm going to head back to my cottage. The day is finally starting to catch up to me. It's shorter if I go this way." Heidi nodded to the path to her left.

Jansen looked down into the eerie darkness. Trees crowded the path, making it hard to see very far along it. He glanced over his shoulder to the path that Heidi had indicated for him. The trees had been cut back to allow more room and more light in.

"Are you sure that you will be okay going that way alone?" Jansen asked as he turned back to look at Heidi. "It looks awfully dark that way. And the path isn't too clear."

Heidi chuckled softly at Jansen's feigned fear. "It's okay. I grew up around here. I know this forest like the back of my hand."

"What about wild animals? All those lions and tigers and bears our parents warned us about when we were young?" Jansen asked. He was standing with his hands on his hips, much like Heidi's father had stood when she was younger and was lecturing her about something she should not have done.

"I don't think that I have to worry about lions and tigers around here. And the bears usually don't come this close to the town," Heidi reasoned. The concern that Jansen was showing her warmed her insides. She missed having someone worry about her and look out for her.

"Still…" Jansen hesitated. It was obvious that he was not comfortable with leaving Heidi alone in the forest at night.

Heidi tried to keep the mood light as nervousness began to creep into her consciousness. It would be too easy to take Jansen's hand and let him lead her back to the inn. She could not risk letting her guard down and letting someone take care of her for one second. She could not trust herself or her reaction. Dean had loved taking care of her. She was not ready yet to let someone else take his place. "I think you're the one I should be more worried about. Are you sure that you'll be able to make it back?"

"Of course." Jansen puffed out his chest and flexed his arms in a show of bravado. "Nothing could scare me. I laugh in the face of danger!" Jansen threw his head back and laughed three, deep, throaty ha, ha, ha's.

Heidi smiled at Jansen, shaking her head slightly. "Well, then, Mr. Wilderness Hero, I will leave you to the wiles of the trees."

Jansen grabbed Heidi's hand before she turned away to head into the trees. He searched Heidi's face before asking softly, "Can I see you tomorrow?"

The look on Jansen's face caused Heidi to catch her breath. It was an intense look. Even though it was dark in the trees, she could see that his eyes had darkened with desire as sparks ignited between their joined hands.

Butterflies fluttered in her stomach. It took a moment before Heidi could find her voice. With an indifferent shrug that she hoped made her look like she did not care either way, Heidi said, "Well, I live here now so I'm sure we'll see each other around."

Heidi turned quickly and fled down the path. Jansen watched until the trees had swallowed her into their darkness. Then, he headed down his path back to the main inn and to his room.

Jansen flipped through the papers one more time before pulling the desk phone towards himself. He punched in a number that he knew by memory and listened as the phone rang on the other end. Impatiently, Jansen drummed his fingers against the polished oak surface of the desk as he waited for someone to pick up.

"Fellows," answered a deep voice after the fifth ring, just before the answering service was scheduled to pick up. The sound of loud music and loud voices could be heard in the background.

"Gord, it's me," said Jansen. "I was just checking in. To see if anything was happening."

"Heah buddy!" Gord said brightly. Jansen could hear the background noise drop a few levels as Gord moved to a quieter corner of the bar. "Glad to see you haven't forgot us all down here slaving away while you're kicking it back in paradise!"

"Humph! I'd rather be down there any day. You know it's killing me sitting up here on my hands." Jansen ran his fingers through his hair and shrugged his shoulders as if it was Gord's image staring back at him in the mirror instead of his own.

"I know, buddy. I know. But it just isn't a good situation down here right now for you. We just can't risk losing you. It would set us back too far. And we're just too close right now to risk anything."

Jansen sighed heavily. It was the same argument that ran through his head every minute of the day trying to convince that other part of him that hated to be out of the line of fire. "Any word as to when the deal will be sealed?"

"Nothing concrete. But we've all got our fingers crossed hoping that it will be soon." Gord tried to sound optimistic but Jansen could tell that Gord was just as worried and frustrated about the progress of the deal as he was. Things had been moving too slowly for some time now. Everyone had been holding their breath, waiting for the slightest movement to set off the explosion.

"It's gotta happen soon. It's been too long since the last one." Jansen slammed his fist in frustration on top of the pile of papers.

Gord interrupted Jansen before he could go any further in his tirade, "Look. I hate to run man but the ladies are a-callin'. I'll keep you posted."

Jansen knew that someone must have come along, preventing Gord from talking any further. It was their signal to each other that they were no longer alone. He did not try to press Gord for more information though he desperately wanted to. Instead, he swallowed his anger and let Gord go. "Okay. Thanks man. You know where you can reach me."

"Yup. And enjoy the scenery!" Gord called cheerily before hanging up.

Jansen sighed as he returned the phone to its cradle. He hated to be so far away, so far from the action. He always liked to be right in the heart of it all. But he knew that it was just too risky for him right now. They were so close, so very close. He just had to try and be patient.

Jansen looked down at the glossy photo in front of him on the desk. A smiling Heidi stared back. Her eyes sparkled with mischievousness. It was a picture from a better time. Maybe if he concentrated on bringing that sparkle back into Heidi's eyes, he could survive the wait.

Chapter Five

The morning sun streamed in through the open curtains, illuminating the sleeping body in a halo of yellow. Heidi groaned and buried herself deeper under the covers. She hid her head under a pillow in an attempt to block out the bright morning light. Finally, she gave up and threw the covers off. She grabbed a lavender terry robe and padded out to the kitchen.

Heidi sighed at the sight that greeted her. Half empty boxes and packing papers littered the floor. Every inch of the countertops and the table were filled with dishes, knickknacks, and picture frames. The movers had come late in the afternoon and Heidi had set about unpacking until she had fallen, exhausted, into her bed at two o'clock in the morning. She had felt the sudden need to surround herself with familiar things.

"Hello in there!" a voice called as the door opened. Gladys entered the cottage and stuck her head in the kitchen. She was wearing a hot pink jogging suit that hugged every curve and had a matching sweatband around her head and each wrist. "Oh my! It looks like a tornado blew through here."

"Good morning, Mom...er...Gladys," Heidi greeted her mother. "I got a little caught up in unpacking last night." She weeded her way through the boxes to the counter and reached for the coffee pot. The last thing she had done before falling into bed last night was set the timer on the coffee maker so there would be fresh coffee waiting for her when she got up. As she filled a mug, Heidi asked, "Would you like some coffee?"

"Please. It's my one sin that I just can't break." Gladys dug a chair out from under a pile of newsprint and perched on its padded seat. "I thought that the movers were supposed to unpack everything."

"I wanted to do it myself." Heidi shrugged. She had sent the packers away shortly after they had unloaded all the boxes and furniture into the rooms that Heidi had indicated. "I'm not sure where I'm going to put everything yet. I have too much stuff for this little cottage."

"Well, why don't you sell it all and start fresh? Buy something new," Gladys suggested. "We could go on a major shopping spree and totally redo everything in this place. Oh, what fun that would be!"

"Hmmm..." Heidi busied herself pouring coffee into two large mugs to avoid answering. When she set the mugs on the table and took a seat across from Gladys, she tried to change the subject. "You're dressed pretty splashy this morning. You look like you're ready to run a marathon."

"I've taken up running," Gladys said. She sat up a little

straighter and sucked in her already flat stomach a little more. "A body like mine just doesn't happen on its own. It takes a lot of work and care. I run about three miles a day now. Do you still run?"

Heidi blanched. She quickly looked down at her coffee mug to hide the look of panic in her eyes. She whispered, "No. Not for awhile now."

"Oh, hon. I'm such a clod." Gladys reached over and gently squeezed Heidi's hand. "I can be so insensitive sometimes. Please forgive me."

"It's okay, Gladys. Maybe I'll start again and join you on your runs." Heidi stood up and reached for the half-full coffee pot. "Would you like some more coffee?"

Gladys held up her hand and shook her head, causing her copper curls to bounce. "No, thanks. I've already had three cups this morning. Five is my daily limit so I have to pace myself."

"Only five?" Heidi raised an eyebrow in her mother's direction. She was not sure if she was hearing right. "I remember when you used to drink coffee like it was water. You always had a cup in your hand."

"Yes, and I can only imagine what all that caffeine has done to me. Natasha has me on a strict diet and only allows me five cups of caffeine of any kind a day."

"Natasha?" Heidi asked, arching one eyebrow up in question.

"She's my nutritionist," Gladys explained. "She runs a small health food store in town. Opened it up about five years ago. And she helps to plan our menus. We have our guests' health in our best interest and only serve food that's good for them."

"Wow! What brought on this sudden concern for your health?"

"I'm getting older you know and this is the time that health problems start developing. I woke up one day and realised that I had better change my ways or I would end up in the hospital tied to a machine."

"So you've started eating healthy and exercising. Think it will help so late in the game?" Heidi smirked slightly. Her mother would not appreciate the dig about her age. She had always worried about getting old.

Gladys chose to ignore the remark and change the subject. "Enough about me now. Did my eyes see right? Did you leave with Jansen after dinner last night?"

"He asked me to take him for a tour of the place," Heidi said simply. She did not want to encourage her mother or her meddling ways with any more details than absolutely necessary.

"Isn't he a dish? He's enough to make an iceberg melt," Gladys gushed like a teenage girl.

"Mother!" exclaimed Heidi. She was shocked at the way her mother was drooling over the man. It was so unlike the prim, reserved woman that she remembered as a child. Things had definitely changed around her childhood home, and more than just the resort and new health kick. Her mother was acting like a teenager on a hormone overdose. Did women have midlife crises? Heidi suddenly felt old. "He's half your age."

"Oh! Not for me hon. I like my men a little more aged, like a great steak. I was meaning for you."

"I am not interested in any relationship right now, Mother." Heidi glared across the table at Gladys to get her point across.

Gladys waved off Heidi's objections as if they were a fly buzzing around her head. "It doesn't have to be a relationship. More like a summer fling. He's a guest here so it's not like he'll be around forever."

"I am not interested in any flings so you can just stop right there," Heidi said with only half-hearted conviction. She definitely did not want to partake in any sort of fling. She had never been able to have just a casual relationship with anyone and she did not think that she would be starting anytime soon. But she just could not dismiss the thought of Jansen quite so easily. Something about him had snagged her senses and would not let go. "You don't even know him. He could be married. Or an escaped convict on the run. Or a murderer! You could be trying to fix up your only child up with a serial killer."

"Oh, Heidi. Don't be so dramatic. You can be so imaginative sometimes. You know really should try your hand at writing. I bet you would be great at it," Gladys suggested.

"I would love to continue this delightful conversation," said Heidi, sarcasm filling her voice, as she picked up the empty cups and put them in the sink, "but I still have a lot of unpacking to do. You can stay and help if you want."

Gladys wrinkled her nose and stood up from the table. She said, "I think I'll pass this morning. I really should be getting back and helping Natasha with the menu for next week. She can sometimes go a little over board with her health food. We want our guests to enjoy the food, not be turned off from food altogether. I'll see you later then. Nana's cooking up some of her famous grilled trout for dinner if you're interested in joining us again."

The silence enveloped Heidi after her mother left. It was a welcome feeling after her mother's insistent chatter and high energy. Heidi sighed as she looked around her. It was going to be another long, hard day of unpacking.

Chapter Six

A sharp knock on the door interrupted Heidi as she pulled crystal candlesticks out of the box beside her. She glanced at the ornate wood clock she had placed on the mantle. It had been her grandmother's and had been given to Heidi when she passed away. Heidi had loved tinkering with it whenever she had visited her grandmother.

The black metal hands showed eight forty-five. Heidi had not realised that is was so late. She had been so wrapped up in unpacking her memories that she did not notice the time flying by.

It's probably Gladys wondering if I am still alive, thought Heidi as she went to the door. She smiled as she pictured Gladys worked up about where she had been all day. She was still chuckling softly to herself when she pulled the door open.

"What's so funny?" asked her visitor. "Do I have something on my face?"

"Oh!" The deep voice startled Heidi. Her heart skipped a couple of beats when she looked up into twinkling brown eyes. "Jansen. It's you."

"You sound so disappointed. Were you expecting someone else?" Jansen looked behind him, trying to see if someone else was coming up the walk after him. When he could not see anyone, he turned back to Heidi and shrugged in apology.

"I...I just thought it was Gladys coming to see if I was buried under a mountain of packing paper and needed rescuing," stammered Heidi, slightly flustered by the man standing at her door. Unconsciously, she twisted a stray lock of hair around her finger, a habit she had when she was nervous.

"She's a little tied up right now. Some kind of kitchen emergency or something. So she sent the backup. I brought some dinner with me." Jansen held up the picnic basket that he was carrying. "I didn't see you at breakfast or lunch so I thought you might be a little hungry."

Heidi's stomach growled at the mention of food. It reminded her that she had not eaten anything since last night, just in case Heidi was thinking of declining Jansen's offer. "Thank you. Come in. I got so wrapped up in unpacking that I forgot to stop and eat. The movers dropped everything off late yesterday afternoon and I've been trying to dig my way out of the mountain of boxes ever since."

Jansen looked around him as he set the basket on the table. He began pulling out plastic dishes of food. "Looks like you've been busy. All this stuff going to fit?"

"No. There's lots of duplicates. Especially since Gladys

had already stocked the place with all the essentials. Most of it will probably go into storage until I either get my own place or decide to sell it," Heidi explained as she followed Jansen into the kitchen.

"Planning to leave already are you?" asked Jansen, an eyebrow arching up as if to accentuate his question.

"No. Just thinking ahead," Heidi said as she took plates and cutlery out of the cupboard. "Life just has a habit of taking a left turn every now and then when a person least expects it."

"It sounds like you're talking from experience."

"A little. Let's eat in the living room," Heidi suggested, quickly diverting Jansen's attention to another subject. "The chairs are more comfortable and a lot less crowded. I think I can actually find them without too much trouble."

Heidi picked up her plate and headed out of the kitchen. Jansen finished filling his plate and followed her into the living room. They settled on opposite ends of the pale blue couch and ate in silence with their plates balanced on their knees.

Heidi did not realise how hungry she was until she took the first bite of her grilled trout. Her stomach rumbled blissfully at the taste. It was a blend of tangy lemon and fine herbs. The wild rice and grilled vegetable medley that accompanied the fish added to the ecstasy of the meal for Heidi. She had almost forgotten what a wonderful cook Nana was. It had been too long since she had been home last.

Jansen watched as Heidi savoured her dinner. She seemed to melt with every bite. An image flitted through his head—an image of Heidi melting under his kisses and caresses, the same look of rapture etched on her face. Her skin would be as smooth as cream and as soft as a goose down pillow. Instead of the fish eliciting those soft little moans from her, it would be his hands and his mouth as he explored the secrets of her body. He felt himself harden as the scene played out. Worried that Heidi might see his reaction, Jansen shifted slightly and moved his plate to cover more of his lap. He took several deep breaths to slow the blood racing through his veins.

Heidi did not notice the effect that she was having on Jansen. She was too wrapped up in enjoying every morsel to the fullest. When the last piece was safely tucked away, she sighed contentedly. She wiped the corners of her mouth with a paper napkin and place the empty plate on the corner of the coffee table. Jansen continued to eat.

Heidi glanced shyly at Jansen sitting at the opposite end of the couch. He was just putting the last piece of fish into his mouth. She said, "Sorry about that. I didn't realise how hungry I was. And it's been awhile since I had such a great meal."

"You don't cook?" asked Jansen. He placed his plate on the coffee table and turned to face Heidi, stretching his arm out along the back of the couch.

Heidi shook her head gently. "I try to avoid it as much as possible. I am a terrible cook. Even with all of Nana's vain attempts. No matter how hard she tried, I could just never get it right. I can even burn water if I try!"

A smile spread across Jansen's face. He covered his mouth and pretended to cough, but it was not enough to prevent the laugh from escaping. The rich baritone notes sent shivers through Heidi's body. They sparked something in Heidi that had been dormant for a long time now.

The laughter was infectious. Soon Heidi found herself laughing, too, which only caused Jansen to laugh harder. In no time, they were both laughing so hard that tears streamed down their faces.

Finally, clutching her sides, Heidi gained enough control of herself to beg, "Please stop. I can't breathe anymore."

"Sorry about that. I just couldn't help it. Haven't heard anyone admit to being able to burn water. Toast, yes. Water, no." Jansen wiped tears from his eyes with his shirtsleeve.

"That's okay," Heidi gasped. She gulped in large lungfuls of air in an attempt to return her breathing back to normal. "It does sound kind of funny when I think about it. It's been awhile since I laughed so hard."

"You should laugh more often. Your eyes are beautiful when they sparkle," Jansen said softly, all traces of laughter gone from his voice.

Heidi glanced down at her hands. She did not know how to respond. It had been a long time since someone had paid her a compliment that was not laced with pity. An uncomfortable silence filled the space between Heidi and Jansen.

Spotting the empty dishes on the coffee table in front of her, Heidi latched onto them as a way to break free of the tension. She stood up, picking the plates up on her way. She asked over her shoulder as she carefully stacked everything together, "Would you like something to drink? I think I saw a bottle of wine in the fridge this morning."

"Sure, but only if it isn't any trouble."

Jansen watched as Heidi took the dishes to the kitchen. He swore softly under his breath at his carelessness. He knew that Heidi's emotional state was still very fragile right now. He had to be very careful that he did not push her too hard or too fast.

When Heidi returned to the livingroom with the bottle of white wine and two glasses, Jansen was standing in front of the fireplace admiring the clock on the mantle. "This is a very beautiful clock," he said, running his fingers lightly over the surface. "It has such fine detail."

"It used to be my grandma's," Heidi explained. She carefully poured wine into each glass and handed one to Jansen. "I used to love playing with it when I was a little girl. Every time I went to visit her, I would spend hours tinkering with it and pretending that I was a clock maker."

Jansen took a sip of wine as he continued to admire the clock. His gaze strayed over to the antique silver frame resting beside it. It held a picture of a handsome young man. He had curly blond hair that just brushed his collar, crystal blue eyes that sparkled with an emotion that could only be described as love, and an animated smile that showed off a perfect row of white teeth. Jansen stared at the picture for a moment. A stab of pain settled deep within his stomach. So much had happened to change that face.

Jansen shook himself from his reverie. He cleared his throat and turned back to where Heidi stood watching him. "I should be going now. You probably have some more unpacking that you want to get done tonight."

"Actually, I was thinking of taking a break for the night. I need to take some of this extra stuff out of here before I do too much more so I can see what I have already and what I have room left for." Heidi waved at the pile of boxes sitting near the front door. "I was thinking of making some popcorn and watching a movie. Care to join me?"

"Sure, if you don't mind the company."

After popping a bag of popcorn in the microwave and drizzling a healthy serving of butter over the top, Heidi flipped through the television channels until they found a movie that neither of them had seen yet. She curled up beside Jansen on the couch and they began to watch the movie in silence. Halfway through the show, Jansen looked over at Heidi and saw that she had fallen asleep. Her head had lolled back against the couch and her mouth was open slightly. A thin line of drool glistened from the corner of her mouth.

She must have been more tired than she realized, Jansen thought. He sat watching Heidi sleep for a few more minutes. He wondered if she was dreaming of anything and if it was of happier times. Or maybe she had worked herself so hard today that she was even too exhausted to dream.

I wish it was me filling her dreams. The thought came out of no where, startling Jansen. He shook his head in an attempt to rid himself of that idea. He was here to check on Heidi, to make sure she was alright, not to seduce her. He did not need a woman complicating his life right now. His life was too dangerous to bring someone into it. He could not put someone so close to harms way, especially not someone as sweet and beautiful as Heidi. And who had already lost so much for reasons beyond her control. He had to stop his mind, and his heart, before it got away from him.

Jansen gently laid Heidi down on the couch and covered her with a knit afghan he found on the armchair. After turning off the television and the lights, Jansen bent over Heidi and kissed her softly on the forehead.

"Good night, angel," he whispered. "Sweet dreams."

Jansen tiptoed out of the cottage, locking the door behind him. Heidi nestled into the softness of the cushions, sighing happily. Peace washed over her face.

Chapter Seven

The dining room was almost empty when Heidi pushed through the door. Only a few of the tables had anyone sitting at them. Most of the early risers were enjoying the morning paper over a cup of coffee or were talking quietly among themselves about the day's plans.

Heidi looked around the room for a familiar face. Though she would prefer to eat alone, her good manners would not let her walk by without acknowledging an acquaintance. In the far corner, in front of one of the floor length windows looking out over the rose gardens, Jansen sat flipping through a pile of papers. He was oblivious to the room around him as he puzzled over the pages in front of him. The morning sun wrapped his shoulders in a soft blanket of sunshine. The red highlights in his dark hair picked up the sun's rays and, as when Heidi first met him, created a halo around his head.

Jansen was dressed in a mustard-coloured T-shirt that stretched snugly across his well-developed upper body and a pair of dark coloured jeans that hugged his long legs. Heidi's heart skipped a couple of beats and her pulse doubled in time. She tingled all over. An image of her and Jansen's naked bodies twined together among the ferns flitted through her mind. She could feel the heat spread through her body as the scene played out in her head. Her breathing became more shallow and ragged.

"Excuse me, ma'am," a voice from behind her broke into her revere.

Heidi spun around, startled. Standing in front of her was a deeply tanned, solidly built man. He towered over her, even though she, herself, was only a few inches under six feet. His sculptured body was clothed in dark blue dress pants and a crisp white shirt. The first two buttons of the shirt were open, revealing a spattering of golden hair curling just below his collarbone, and his shirt sleeves were rolled up to his elbows to show the same golden hair sprinkled over his forearms. The sun streaks in his hair and copper tones to his skin hinted at time spent outdoors.

Heidi looked up into hazel eyes that sparkled with amusement. A stray lock of dirty blonde hair fell across his eyes. The stranger reached up and absently brushed it away.

"Oh!" Heidi stammered. She could feel a blush colouring her cheeks. "I'm sorry. I didn't hear anyone come in behind me. I was just looking for a table to eat breakfast at."

"Well, there seems to be quite an assortment to choose from. But if you're alone, why don't you join me and my friend?" invited the stranger.

"I wouldn't want to interrupt. I don't mind eating alone," Heidi said quickly.

"Nonsense! We would be delighted to have you join us. It would help to brighten up our day."

The stranger gave Heidi a dazzling smile that she could hardly dare refuse. Before she realised what she was doing, she was following the stranger across the room.

"Heah, Jansen! Clear away those boring papers. Look at the pretty little thing I found wandering around looking for company," announced the stranger as he stopped at the table in the far corner.

Jansen looked up at the sound of the voice. He glanced briefly at the man before turning to the newcomer standing slightly behind him. A warm smile broke across his face.

"Good morning, sunshine," greeted Jansen. "I think it is more like the other way around—this pretty little thing has just returned my lost partner."

"Good morning, Jansen," replied Heidi. Suddenly, she felt shy and awkward. If she had known that Jansen was the friend that the stranger was referring to, she would have found any excuse not to join them. She would have found any excuse to run and hide, especially after the thoughts she had just been having about the man. She coloured slightly at the remembered images. Luckily, neither Jansen nor the stranger noticed the deepening red staining her cheeks.

The stranger raised an eyebrow as he looked from Jansen to Heidi, "You two know each other? And fairly well by the looks of it."

"Gord, this is Heidi Murray. Heidi, this is Gord Fellows, my partner," introduced Jansen.

"Nice to meet you Gord. Did you just get in?" Heidi asked.

"I came up this morning to bring some papers to Jansen. I needed his approval on a few things for a project we are working on," Gord explained as he picked up a black leather briefcase from the chair beside Jansen and moved it to the other side of the table.

"If you guys are working, I can go eat somewhere else," Heidi said. She glanced down at the papers spread out in front of Jansen. "I'm sure Gladys is around somewhere and would welcome an interruption."

"No. No. We're done here for now," said Jansen. To prove his point, he quickly began to gather the papers scattered across the table into one pile. He shuffled them together before Heidi could get a good look at them and see what they were about. "And we could use the interruption. Especially such a pleasant one."

"My thoughts exactly," agreed Gord. He pulled out an empty chair between himself and Jansen and indicated for Heidi to sit down.

"Well. If you insist. I'll just go grab something to eat and be right back. Can I bring either of you anything?" asked Heidi as she waved off the offered chair.

Jansen and Gord both shook their heads no. They watched Heidi walk over to the buffet table and begin filling a plate from the wide variety of breakfast foods spread out for the guests to enjoy.

When Heidi was safely out of hearing, Gord turned to his partner. "Heidi Murray? That name sounds familiar…"

"She's from the case," answered Jansen. He stuffed the stack of papers into the briefcase at his feet. He turned back to Gord with a warning, "But don't breathe a word about anything. She doesn't know who I am or what I do."

"You know me better then that. I wouldn't say a word about a case while it's still under investigation," Gord said, a look of innocence on his face. "Even if my partner was nailing one of the key subjects."

"I'm not nailing anyone," Jansen growled.

"Maybe not yet. But you sure want to jump into her pants."

Jansen simply glared menacingly at Gord across the table. Heidi joined them again before Jansen had a chance to reply.

Heidi pushed her plate away, sighing contentedly. The last couple of mouthfuls of her crepe swam in a small puddle of syrup and melting whipped cream. She dabbed at her mouth with a pale blue cloth napkin and tossed it on top of the plate.

"All filled up?" asked Gord, a teasing smile playing at the corners of his mouth.

"I don't think I could eat another bite," said Heidi. She patted her full stomach for emphasis. "It's been a long time since I had Nana's special breakfast fruit crepes."

"I don't think you could eat anymore even if you wanted to," Gord said. He nodded towards the empty buffet table. "I think you cleaned the place all out."

"I did not!" retorted Heidi. She tossed her head and looked down her nose at Gord in mock contempt. "I only had a couple."

Gord snorted, trying to hold back the peal of laughter that threatened to burst out. "Yeah, a couple of dozen."

"Let me see," Jansen joined in on the teasing, "your impressive cooking skills don't stretch beyond water so you can't make Saturday-morning crepes for yourself?"

Heidi could feel her cheeks growing warm. She knew that Jansen was remembering their conversation from last night when she admitted her lack of culinary skills. She said, in mock outrage, "You weren't supposed to say anything about that. Ever. You promised."

Jansen held up his hands as if to ward off an attack. "I didn't say anything. Nothing specific, anyway."

"Are you two going to fill me in," asked Gord, "or just leave me sitting here in the dark?" He looked from Jansen to Heidi, one eyebrow raised in question. "The more the merrier when it comes to fun and games I always say."

Jansen, his eyes never leaving Heidi's rosy face, answered, "Sorry, man. The little lady here swore me to secrecy. It's a promise that I just can't go back on. Not when she's within hearing anyway. Ask me about it later."

"You wouldn't dare!" exclaimed Heidi.

"I see," said Gord. He pretended to look hurt, dabbing at the corner of his eyes with a napkin. "That's the way it is. My best friend and partner, the man who I would do anything for, anything, even travel half way around the world to save his bony butt, is going to turn on me for a woman. Granted the woman is quite a stunner and probably well worth it. But still, that doesn't make up for years upon years of friendship and loyalty."

"I think you'll survive," interrupted Jansen. He rolled his eyes at Gord's theatrics "Maybe we could even find you a nice young lass to soothe your wounded ego while you're here."

"Well now that's an idea." Gord perked up at the thought. He turned to Heidi with a gleam in his eye. "You know anyone who would want to hook up for a short time?"

"How short of time are we talking about?" asked Heidi, sceptically.

"Oh, I don't know." Gord shrugged his shoulders. He gave Heidi a devilish smile and big wink. "Maybe an hour or two. Depends on how long my partner here takes finishing up his work."

"That's it?" exclaimed Heidi.

"What? You don't think that's enough time?" asked Gord, innocently.

"Depends on how well you want to get to know the person," Heidi said. "There's not a whole lot you can find out in a few hours."

Gord winked at Heidi again. "Sweetheart, a few hours is all I need to learn the finer points of a woman's psyche."

"Gord's not much into words," explained Jansen, sending a pointed look in the direction of his partner. "He's more of an action man."

It took a minute before the meaning behind Jansen's words dawned on Heidi. She blushed a deep shade of red when she finally realized what Gord's insinuations really meant.

The bright glow of Heidi's face was not lost on Gord. He hooted softly and slapped Jansen on the back. "We got us an innocent one here, bud. My favourite kind to corrupt!" He rubbed his hands together gleefully.

"Easy now cowboy," said Jansen. "I think Heidi's smart enough not to fall for your sweet talkin'. She's not like the brainless bodies you usually hook up with."

"Well, maybe it's time I start broadening my horizons." Gord rested his chin on his hand and leaned over towards Heidi. He waggled his eyebrows and gave Heidi an exaggerated wink.

"Why don't you start broadening them by going and getting me some more coffee," Jansen said, pushing his empty cup towards Gord. "You could start by serving me for a change. Maybe there's a waitress you can bother along the way."

Gord opened his mouth to say something back but thought better of it when he saw the look of warning on Jansen's face. Instead, he picked up the cup and went in search of more coffee.

After Gord was safely out of earshot, Jansen turned back to Heidi. His smile was sheepish. "Sorry about that. Gord's motto in life is 'lay 'em and leave 'em'. His mom abandoned him when he was young so he has a problem with long term commitments. Even short term commitments sometimes. He can forget to be discreet about his philosophy at times."

Heidi looked in the direction that Gord had went before saying, "It must have been tough on him. But he seems to be a good guy other than that."

"He is," Jansen agreed, wholeheartedly. "He would do anything for a friend. Even without being asked. He would give up everything if it would help."

"What did he mean when he said that he went half way around the world to save a friend? Were you in some kind of trouble that he got you out of?" Heidi asked. She turned back to Jansen, full of curiosity.

Jansen glanced down at the table. He toyed with his spoon, trying to decide how to answer Heidi's question. How much could he tell her without revealing a hint of what he did and causing more questions? Trying to be as vague as he could, he said, "I fell in with some real bad guys a few years back and got into a lot of trouble. Gord saw what was happening and pulled me out before things got too ugly."

"It sounds like you two are close."

"Very. We grew up together and always looked out for each other's backs." There was a wistful note to Jansen's voice.

"It must be nice to have such a close friend. To have someone who knows everything about you and who understands you," Heidi said. She felt a little bit jealous. She had had a friend like that, someone to lean on, someone to watch out for her, someone who knew everything about her and still loved her, faults and all. But he had been stolen from her. Heidi felt her throat tighten at the thought.

"I'm not sure if I would be where I am today if it wasn't for Gord. He helped me get through some pretty rough times," Jansen said. He did not see the effect the conversation was having on Heidi. He did not see her strangled look. Instead, he was seeing his past and the friend who had helped him survive it.

"Heah, you two," said Gord as he returned to the table. He set the full coffee cup in front of Jansen before flopping back down in his chair. "Why the long faces? Did you all miss me that much?"

Jansen snorted. "Don't flatter yourself too much."

"Well, Your Majesty, if you don't need anything else, I should be heading back to the city. Got a long day of work ahead of me. Unlike some people here, I don't have the luxury of goofing off all day. I have to hold down the fort." Gord rose to leave once again. Before he turned away, he said to Heidi, "You look after my boy here, now. Keep an eye on him for me. This one likes to get into a wee bit of trouble every now and then if you don't watch him closely."

"I will," said Heidi. "It was good meeting you Gord. I hope you can come back soon."

"Me too. And maybe next time I'll be able to take a little vacation and sample the local offerings instead of having to work all the time." Gord winked at Heidi. He turned to Jansen before leaving. "I'll keep you posted on how everything goes."

"Thanks, man. Take it easy."

Heidi and Jansen were quiet for a minute as Gord walked away. Shaking herself from her reverie, Heidi began to gather the remnants of the breakfast dishes. She said, "I should get these dishes to the kitchen so they can be washed for lunch."

"What are your plans for the day?" asked Jansen. "More unpacking?"

Heidi heaved a big sigh and shrugged her shoulders. Less than enthusiastically, she answered, "I probably should. The mountain doesn't seem to be getting any smaller. But I just can't seem to make myself start right now."

"Can I interest you in another tour? You've showed me around this place. How about the town now?" Jansen asked hopefully.

Heidi stopped stacking dishes to look at Jansen. He had such a pleading look on his face, like a little boy begging for ice cream, that Heidi could not resist. "Sure. Why not? I can always unpack more tonight. And it would be such a waste of a beautiful day being stuck inside."

"Great!" Jansen jumped up and grabbed the stack of dishes in front of Heidi. "Let's drop these dishes off at the kitchen and go exploring."

Laughing at his enthusiasm, Heidi followed Jansen out of the dining room.

"This is such a quaint little town. So friendly and inviting," exclaimed Jansen as he and Heidi strolled along the quiet street. "I could really get used to living in a place like this."

"It is a definite change from living in the city," said Heidi.

"The pace is so much slower and more laid back. No one is in a big rush."

Heidi and Jansen strolled down one of only two sidewalks in Hadey's Cove. The other one was on the opposite side of the street. Businesses lined up on each side, their windows, like eyes, watching people pass by. The store fronts looked tired and weathered, no matter how many coats of fresh paint were applied in an attempt to brighten up the buildings. Colourful flowers tumbled from clay pots standing sentry beside each door and dotting the sidewalk. They bravely opened their petals skyward as the warm morning sun beat down on them.

The street was busy with people moving from one building to the next doing their morning errands or just browsing through the local wares. Jansen was quick to pick out the local residents; they greeted everyone they passed with a friendly hello whether they knew them or not. Occasionally someone stopped to talk to Heidi, to ask her how she was doing and how she liked being back in town.

Jansen stood slightly apart during these conversations, watching. He could see Heidi grow more and more uncomfortable with all the questions about her welfare and the thinly masked sympathy. An overwhelming desire to protect Heidi from any more pain came over him. He yearned to wrap his arms around her and sweep her away. He watched as Heidi put on a brave face for her neighbours and hide her discomfort behind a bright, forced smile. She did not turn from the people, but simply met them with unwavering courage. Jansen was proud of Heidi for the way she handled herself no matter how much it hurt.

For lunch, Heidi and Jansen dined on garden salads and freshly baked garlic bread at the Hadey's Cove Diner. Small Parisian-style bistro tables and chairs had been set up outside under a bright red and white awning. Single stems of flowers in tiny glass vases bobbed their heads in the gentle breeze. Classical music was piped outside through the speakers discreetly hidden among potted trees placed at the corners of the patio. The dining area had been set up to emulate on open air café in Europe, right down to the stuffy, rude waiter. The inside of the diner, however, took a step back in time to the American rock and roll era of the '50s and '60s with its red vinyl seats, Formica tables, mini-jukeboxes where customers could pick their own favourite classic dinner music, and waitresses in poodle skirts and bobby socks.

Jansen and Heidi joked about the stark contrasts in the two atmospheres as they enjoyed their lunch. Peels of laughter dotted their conversation. The other diners smiled over at them from time to time. They were warmed by the sight of a young couple so obviously smitten with each other.

After finishing their lunch and good-naturedly arguing over who would pay the bill, they continued their tour of the town. Heidi insisted on treating Jansen to a double scoop Rocky Road ice cream cone at the General Store since Jansen had won the argument over paying for lunch.

They stopped to sit on the wooden bench outside the General Store while they ate their ice cream. Heidi entertained Jansen with the local history, pointing out the people, the buildings, and the places in her stories. Her mind, though, was only half on the stories that she was spinning. The rest of her hummed from the sensations caused by Jansen's thigh brushing casually against hers. The air fairly sizzled with the electricity between them. Heidi yearned to run her hand up the length of Jansen's thigh. She yearned to feel the muscles rippling under her touch, to feel their strength and power. She shifted slightly so that her leg was pressed a little more closely against Jansen's. It felt hard and sensual against her side.

Before the feelings could take a greater hold, Heidi jumped up from the bench. She started to move down the sidewalk at a brisk pace, not waiting to see if Jansen was following.

At the end of the block, Heidi and Jansen stopped in front of a greying building. The sign above the door welcomed customers to Henry's Hardware. However, no light spilled from the large plate glass windows to invite customers in. A note on the door said that the store was closed due to illness. A middle-aged woman working behind the counter noticed Heidi and Jansen standing outside and waved them in. Heidi pushed open the glass door, jingling the bells hanging overhead. Stale air greeted them as they entered the dimness.

"Hello, Doris. Where's Henry?" Heidi asked the lady behind the counter. Doris was the town's realtor. She had taken on the job more as a hobby after her children had all left home. With the position, she had become the town's source for the latest, and most accurate, gossip. If someone wanted to know what was happening, he or she went to Doris to find out. She had an uncanny knack for knowing things almost before they happened.

"Hello, dearie," greeted Doris. "It's so nice to have you back in town. Poor Henry slipped on some ice this spring and broke his hip. Doctors have him confined to his bed. As much as they can anyway."

"Must be pretty hard on poor Henry. Never knew him to close the store for anything, except maybe for national holidays. And then more just because he said it was his patriotic duty to do so," Heidi said. She moved over to the counter to talk with Doris and catch up on the latest gossip around town.

"Yes, it has been tough," agreed Doris. "The doctors had to practically tie him down for the first little while."

"Isn't there anyone to run the store until he gets better?" Heidi asked.

"No, unfortunately not." Doris said sadly. She gave her head a slight shake for emphasis. "Henry's kids are scattered all across this country and are all so busy with their own lives. The youngest boy, Karl, wants Henry to come live with him in the city."

"That's too bad. What's going to happen to the store?"

"Henry told me this morning to try and sell it."

While Heidi caught up on the rest of the town gossip with Doris, Jansen wandered around the store. He drifted among the isles piled high with tools and gadgets and everything else imaginable for the budding carpenter.

There were even a few articles that could not even be imagined. Only an old school carpenter would know what they were or what to use them for. At the rear of the store were bins of nails and screws in every shape and size. An old, dry measure scale stood in the corner to weigh out the goods. Jansen marvelled at the variety of items on display. The store hinted of a bygone era when the hardware store was a small town staple.

As he moved back up the isles, a large showcase at the front of the store caught Jansen's attention. He knelt in front of the dusty case and stared at the intricately carved figures inside. There were animals of different shapes and sizes and in different poses. Each one had been individually hand carved so no two figures were alike. Cards tucked among the figures gave the name of the local artist and a brief biography.

Heidi turned and watched Jansen in front of the showcase. The afternoon sun slanted in through the plate glass window, surrounding him in a circle of light. The rays cast a warm glow over his face and danced among the highlights in his hair. Heidi felt her breath catch and her heartbeat quicken. A burning heat sparked low in her abdomen and fanned out across her body. Desire rippled through her veins.

Heidi shook herself slightly. She should not be feeling this way. Could not. She turned her attention back to the lady behind the counter. "Sorry, Doris. I wasn't paying attention. Must have been daydreaming for a minute.

What were you saying?"

"I was just commenting on how good that man looks over there," Doris said as she nodded towards Jansen still kneeling in front of the showcase. "He looks like a Roman god or something with the sun coming in like that."

"Oh, Doris. You have such an imagination." Heidi shivered slightly. Doris had just voiced the thought that had flitted through her mind.

"Come now, dearie. Don't tell me you wouldn't jump at the chance to spend a night rolling around in the hay with him."

Chapter Eight

Jansen looked up from his morning paper to watch three young girls, pigtails bouncing, chase around a large blue beach ball across the lawn. They giggled and squealed in delight as they tried to keep it from touching the ground without using their hands.

Jansen smiled as he watched the girls. He had always dreamed of having a house full of kids one day but had put any thoughts of a family on hold when he had started his job at the agency. Things could be dangerous enough without having to worry about a family being caught in the crossfire. He had seen enough families get torn apart by the dangers of the job to not want to intentionally put anyone in that position himself. Maybe it was time to start thinking about a career change and settling down. He was getting older and he did want to have kids while he was still young enough to enjoy them.

A flash of colour at the edge of the trees caught Jansen's eye. Immediately, his training kicked in and he became more alert. He shifted in his chair so he could better see the forest without being obvious. At the same time, he silently chastised himself for not being more alert. Just because he was on vacation did not mean that he should let his guard down. Not when danger was still out there. His heart picked up its pace as he tried to see who, or what, was lurking around. Just as Jansen was about to move closer to take a better look, Heidi stepped out from among the trees. She paused briefly, as if unsure whether or not to continue on.

Jansen's breath caught in his throat when he saw Heidi standing in front of the backdrop of towering pine trees. She was wearing a gauzy cotton shirt and cut-off jean shorts. The shirt was of the palest green colour and seemed to caress her skin like a lover's hand as it rippled and waved in the soft breeze. A pang of jealousy shot through Jansen. He wanted to be the one wrapping Heidi in a silky embrace, to feel her smooth skin under his touch. The breeze picked up lightly and fluttered through Heidi's hair. She had left it to fall in red waves down her back.

Jansen watched as Heidi joined in on the girls' game after making her way across the wide lawn. Her laugh drifted up to him as she tried to bump the ball back into the air with her knee. It sounded like a thousand tinkling bells on a clear frosty winter morning. An overwhelming desire coursed through Jansen's body, causing vessels to contract and blood to pool. He shifted in his chair to try to relieve some of the tightness in his groin.

Heidi played with the girls for a few more minutes before

leaving them to their game. She turned towards the house and slowly climbed the steps to the veranda. There was still a faint smile on her lips.

"Good morning, sunshine!" called Jansen, startling Heidi out of her thoughts.

"Oh!" Heidi exclaimed as she looked around her to find out where the voice had come from. Finally she spotted Jansen sitting in the shadows at one of the white wicker tables scattered along the veranda. "Jansen. Good morning. I didn't see you there."

"Sorry to scare you like that," Jansen apologized, a smile lighting his face.

"Oh, you didn't scare me," Heidi interrupted quickly. Her heart was beating wildly and she felt flustered all of a sudden. "I just wasn't expecting anyone to be out here still. I thought everyone would be out enjoying the day already."

"I was just sitting here catching up on the morning news and trying to decide what I would like to do first. There are just too many choices."

"Oh. Well, I'll leave you to your paper then. I should go check and see if Gladys needs any help with anything." Heidi turned and quickly moved to the front doors. She tried to open the door but it wouldn't budge. Glancing over at Jansen, she laughed nervously, "Old doors. They like to stick sometimes."

Jansen smiled at Heidi. He could tell that something had her worked up and wondered what it could be. Was his sitting here having an effect on her? He knew that he should not read anything into it, but his chest puffed up a little bit just the same.

"Um, I think the door opens in, not out," Jansen suggested.

A deep red stained Heidi's cheeks as the door opened easily with an inward push. She mumbled a quick thank you before diving through it. She leaned against the cool wood after pushing it closed behind her. Taking several deep breaths, Heidi tried to calm her racing heart.

What is the matter with me? thought Heidi. Why am I so worked up? It's just Jansen. A regular guest at the house just like everyone else. There should be no reason to be so nervous. Why do I feel like a teenager with my first crush whenever I'm around him?

Even though Heidi had only known him for a few days, there was something about the man that sent her emotions into a whirlwind and her hormones into overdrive. She had not been able to sleep much last night. Had not been able to sleep much since she returned to Hadey's Cove, in fact. Every time she had closed her eyes, a tall, athletic man with dark wavy hair and soul-searching eyes flooded her dreams.

That must be my problem this morning, Heidi thought. All I need is a little more sleep and I'll be okay. Maybe if I can just keep myself busy I'll feel better and wear myself out enough to get a good sleep tonight.

Heidi pushed herself away from the door and went in search of her mother and something to distract her mind from the handsome man sitting on the veranda.

"Jansen! What a lovely surprise to see you out here," greeted Gladys as she approached his table. "Now what is such a handsome young man like yourself doing sitting all alone?"

"Good morning, Gladys," Jansen greeted in return. He shuffled together the morning paper that he had been trying to read and indicated the empty chair beside him. "Care to join me?"

"I would be delighted. I never turn down an invitation from a young man. They just don't come along often enough anymore to be picky," Gladys said as she settled herself into the empty wicker chair. She crossed her long legs, brushing against Jansen's in the process.

Gladys was dressed in a loud floral print shirt and body-hugging orange Capri pants. Her copper hair had been pulled back into a messy ponytail and secured with a large plastic flower clip. Everything about the woman screamed attention.

"I hope I wasn't interrupting anything," Gladys said as she nodded towards the folded paper beside Jansen.

Jansen looked over in the direction of Gladys' glance. He shook his head and said, "No. I was just finishing up on the morning news."

"Anything interesting out there in the big wide world today?"

"Nothing much besides the usual mugging, robbery, and deceitful politician promising something that he can never deliver."

Gladys chuckled softly. She batted playfully at Jansen. Her orange, manicured nails scratched lightly across the bare skin of his fore arm. "I see living in the city hasn't made you the least bit cynical."

"Not one bit," said Jansen, smiling. He shifted slightly in his chair, trying to move as far away from Gladys as he could without actually getting up and moving to another table. The woman made him a little bit uncomfortable with her over-the-top flirting and flamboyant style. He turned and looked over the grounds in an attempt to find something to change the subject and deflect the attention away from him. "You have a beautiful place here. Very peaceful and refreshing."

"Thank you. It is my pride and joy. Everything I have has gone into making this place succeed," Gladys said, a wistful note filling her voice.

"Heidi said that you changed the house over into an inn a few years ago."

"It's been about fifteen years now I guess since I first opened the inn. Though it does only seem like yesterday somedays," Gladys explained. She nervously twisted the washcloth in her hands. She looked out across the wide yard as she continued. "After my husband died, I could hardly afford the upkeep on the place. And it just broke my heart to even think about moving from here into something smaller. So it was either invite strangers into my house or lose it all."

"It looks like you have been a success."

"It was been a long, hard fought success. The first years were a little tough. It took all my savings and most of my husband's life insurance money to renovate the house to meet building codes and put in all new industrial sized appliances in the kitchen. And then came the problem of trying to convince people to come out to the middle of no where for a holiday. Lucky for us, the town threw themselves behind us and created more tourist attractions.

It has been a lot of hard work and sleepless nights. But it has been worth it all. The first few years were pretty lean but we have been able to collect a fairly large, faithful clientele that have helped to pay the bills. I wouldn't change things for the world. I love doing this. I love looking after people. It's like having friends visit all the time." Turning back to Jansen, Gladys smiled sweetly and turned the topic away from her. "But enough about me. What keeps you busy in the city?"

Heidi glanced out the window that she was absently washing. She watched two squirrels chasing each other up and down the front railing. Their insistent chatter could barely be heard through the glass. Heidi smiled to herself. How much easier life would be if she was a squirrel with only having to worry about where her next supply of nuts was coming from.

Heidi picked up her spray bottle and moved over to the next window. After a liberal spritzing of cleaner, she began to wipe off the glass in large sweeping circles. She slowly made her way around the front room until she stood in front of a window overlooking the side veranda. She stopped in mid-spray when she saw her mother lean over to Jansen and rest a hand on his arm. The two looked very cosy sitting there enjoying the morning sun together.

A pang of jealousy hit Heidi. She wanted to be the one laughing at what Jansen was saying. She wanted to be the one holding his attention. She wanted to be the one fawning over him.

What am I thinking? thought Heidi, shaking herself. I don't want any of that. I'm content being alone. And I have to remember Dean. I can't let anything fade his memory. No one will ever take his place in my life or my heart. I owe him that much.

Heidi shook her head to clear out any further thoughts of Jansen, picked up her cleaning supplies, and headed back to the cleaning closet. There had to be something else that she could do to keep her mind busy. Something in the back corner of the house that needed to be done. Somewhere where there would be no chance of running into any guests, one in particular.

"Well, Jansen. It was nice talking to you but I really should get back to work. Heidi will think that I deserted her," said Gladys as she pushed her chair away from the table. She paused before walking away and turned back to Jansen. She studied him closely for a minute before saying, "I really hope you will be able to reach Heidi. She needs someone to bring her back into the land of the living. It's time she stopped mourning and get on with her life. Just don't hurt her. She's been hurt enough already."

Jansen watched as Gladys disappeared into the house before turning his attention to the activities on the lawn in front of him. He was soon lost in his thoughts. Gladys had given him a valuable insight into Heidi. Now, he just had to figure out how to use this information to get closer to the woman who filled his dreams of late.

Chapter Nine

Heidi pushed open the door of the diner, sending the tiny bells overhead jingling. She glanced around the almost-empty restaurant in search of her grandfather. For as long as she could remember, he had been meeting three of his buddies for breakfast every Monday morning. It was an unspoken date between the four friends that had started when they were all young men with new families and new jobs. At first, the Monday morning breakfasts were a chance for the friends to meet and get away from the everyday pressures of the supporting their families. As their families grew and the friends moved on into retirement, the breakfast had evolved into a griping and gossip session. They argued over whose aches and pains were the worst and discussed the newest rumours around town.

Grandpa was enjoying a last cup of coffee in a booth with a view of both the diner and the street outside. His back was to the door so he did not see Heidi approach his table.

"Good morning Grandpa," Heidi greeted him cheerfully. She leaned down to place a soft kiss on his weathered cheek. "Mind if I join you?"

"Oh, Heidi!" Grandpa said, surprised. He quickly piled up the few remaining dishes from breakfast and gestured to the empty bench across from him. "Of course you can. I always have time for my favourite granddaughter."

"I'm you're only granddaughter," laughed Heidi. She picked up a laminated menu from the stand on the end of the table and flipped it over to the breakfast offerings.

Grandpa chuckled too. It was a long-standing joke between them. "Yeah, but you're still my favourite."

A middle-aged woman with frizzy platinum hair, a pencil stuck behind her ear, and a half-empty coffeepot in her hand bustled by to the table. "Mornin', Heidi. What can I get you this morning, darlin'?"

Heidi took one last look at the menu before setting it aside and turning towards the waitress. "Good morning, Jeannie. I'll have the Sunrise Special, eggs over easy, bacon, and whole wheat toast. And a small glass of orange juice."

"Coming right up, dear," said Jeannie. She topped up Grandpa's cup before heading back to the kitchen with Heidi's order.

Grandpa measured in a heaping teaspoon of sugar and poured a generous helping of cream into his coffee cup. He gave everything a swirl, the sound of metal clanking against ceramic echoing in the nearly empty diner. "So what do I owe this special treat to? I thought you would still be settling in."

"I came to town to see about renting a storage room for some of my stuff. It seems that I have more things than room. So I thought I would store anything I have extra of for now while I decide what I'm going to do with everything."

"My basement is empty. Why don't you store your extra stuff down there?" suggested Grandpa. He blew steam from his coffee before taking a generous gulp.

Heidi started to protest but stopped. Even though he was trying to hide behind his coffee cup, Heidi could see the hope in her grandfather's face. Heidi had been very close to him when she was growing up and after her father died, they had grown even closer. Whenever she had needed a break from her mother, Heidi had run to her grandfather's house. They would go fishing or to a ballgame until things had not looked so unbearable anymore.

Heidi could almost see the thoughts bouncing around her grandfather's head. He was forever scheming. By using his basement for storage, Heidi would still have a reason to visit him. Instead of calling him on it, Heidi decided to accept her grandfather's offer. "If you think you have enough room. I don't want to impose on you or clutter your house with all my junk."

"Nonsense." Grandpa waved his hand at Heidi, chasing away any more objections before she could voice them. "I have plenty of room. And since I wasn't there to help move you, this is the least I can do. You shouldn't have to spend your money on storage when I have a half-empty house you can fill up for free. And maybe there'll be something in your pile that I can use."

"If you're absolutely sure," Heidi said. She did not want to give in too easily and give away the fact that she knew her grandfather's plan. "I've got a bunch of boxes and small furniture ready to move out of my house. I'll come by later today or tomorrow to drop them off."

"Why don't you use my truck to move everything, too? It will be easier than trying to jam things into your mother's tiny tin box." offered Grandpa. He pushed his empty coffee cup away from him. He dug into his pocket to retrieve his keys and set them on the table in front of Heidi. "George and I are planning on going fishing for a couple of days so I won't be needing my truck. It's George's turn to drive this trip."

Heidi added her empty breakfast dishes to the empty coffee cup before picking up the keys and stuffing them in the pocket of her jeans. "I was hoping I could borrow your truck. There would only be a couple of trips to make instead of a hundred or so if I used Mom's car. I should be done moving things to your place by tomorrow night so I'll just leave your truck in the driveway when I'm done. It'll be ready and waiting for you when you get back."

"Take as long as you want. I have no place important to be for the next while."

Grandpa and Heidi lapsed into a comfortable silence for a few minutes. They watched the shoppers move down the sidewalk from store to store as the sound of clanking dishes filled the diner. Jeannie and the other waitresses were busy cleaning up after the breakfast rush and preparing for the next wave of people looking for lunch.

After a few moments, Grandpa cleared his throat and ventured into a new area of conversation, "You seem to be spending a lot of time with a young fellow staying at the inn. Doris was saying that the two of you were strolling around town the other day and having lunch together."

Heidi mentally sighed. The town gossips were busy at it again. It was the one thing that she had not missed when she had moved away and was one of the things she dreaded about moving back. Everyone would be watching her every move. "I was just showing Jansen around town. He asked for a tour and I was looking for an excuse to get away from unpacking. And I thought it was a good opportunity to see what had changed in town since I was last through here."

"Doris said the two of you looked pretty comfortable together. Like you were having a good time."

Heidi shrugged her shoulders. She toyed with the packets of sugar in the bowl, rearranging them in different patterns instead of meeting her grandfather's gaze. "It was a nice morning. And we get along fairly well. It was nothing more than two people enjoying a walk together."

"Not unless you want it to be something more," suggested Grandpa.

This time Heidi sighed out loud. She had been down this road already with her mother. The arguments were becoming second nature. She could almost spout them off without actually thinking about them. "I am not looking for anything right now. I am okay being by myself right now."

Grandpa rubbed his worn thumb over a chip in the laminate table top. He understood the pain that Heidi was going through but he also knew that she was young and needed to move on with life. She needed to find someone to add some laughter and sunshine back into her life. And he had not been entirely truthful to Heidi about hearing the gossip concerning her and the new man in town. He had watched them for most of the day as they strolled from shop to shop and enjoyed ice cream in front of the General Store. He had seen the easy companionship flow between them. And for a short time, he had seen Heidi happy again. Grandpa's tired bones were telling him that this was the man for Heidi. This was Heidi's second chance at a happy life. Now he just had to give her a push in the right direction.

"A person should never close his eyes to happiness. We were made to live as pairs, not alone."

"What about you, Grandpa?" Heidi tried to divert the attention from her and her love life before Grandpa gathered too much steam. "Why are you still living alone?

It's been quite a few years since Grandma passed away and you're still somewhat of a spring chicken. Where's the other half to your pair?"

"I'm too mean and crusty for anyone to want to live with me. And besides, Grandma spoiled me for all other women. Nobody could ever live up to her now," Grandpa said. He added with a sly little grin, "Besides, just because there ain't no woman in my house doesn't mean I ain't been entertaining. I just don't let them stick around too long. I've been caught once and I don't mean to be caught again. I'm spending my golden years chasing those skirts I missed in my younger days."

"Well, I believe the crusty part. And the spoiled part," said Heidi. Her grandpa and grandma had had the perfect marriage. It was a marriage that Heidi yearned to have herself. Her one chance at it had been stolen from her. She did not believe that she would get a second chance. Nor did she want one right now. Her first marriage had been too precious to risk on another one. There was no way she was lucky enough to have another chance at utter happiness. "And I almost believe the tomcatting part. You're too much of a charmer for your own good."

A smile lit up Grandpa's face. He loved the good-natured bickering that came easily between him and his granddaughter. They could find anything to debate about. Arguing with Heidi made Grandpa feel young and alive again. "We're not talking about my happiness here. I'm too old to change my ways. But you, young lady, still have a lot of years ahead of you. You shouldn't be spending them alone. You need a special someone to share them with. I'm not going to be around forever to keep arguing with you, you know."

It was the same thing that everyone had been telling Heidi. The only thing they could not tell her was how to move on. How to forget about the past. How to forget the pain. Heidi did not have the energy to argue with her grandfather about this. Instead, she focused on the last thing Grandpa had said. "You're stubborn enough to outlast the lot of us, Grandpa. And besides, no one could replace you. I can't think of anyone who could argue as well as you. You could argue yourself out of box if you set your mind to it."

Grandpa chuckled. "You're not half bad yourself sweetheart."

"I learned from the best," Heidi said. She reached over and gave her grandfather's hand a gentle squeeze. Right now, this was the only relationship that Heidi was interested in. Her grandfather was right; he would not be around forever. Heidi wanted to spend time getting to know her grandfather again and making up for all those years when she was away. "You know, it's been awhile since I was fishing. What say that when you get back from fishing with George, you and I plan a trip somewhere? We could do some fishing, maybe a little camping. Just like old times."

Over a fresh pot of coffee, Heidi and her grandfather planned their fishing trip. They reminisced about past trips and the ones that got away. They argued over who caught the most fish and what the best bait was. They continued to talk as the diner filled up around them with the lunch crowd. Finally, when they started telling the same stories over again, Heidi drove her grandfather home and headed back to her cottage in the trees, alone.

Chapter Ten

Heidi had just finished putting the last cardboard box into the back of her grandfather's truck and was stretching to get the kinks out of her back when she saw someone coming through the trees. She shaded her eyes from the bright afternoon sun to get a better look. She watched as the figure came closer.

Heidi recognized the man before he cleared the stand of trees. It was Jansen. She could tell by his walk and the way he carried himself. His back was rigid yet he walked loose-limbed as if he expected someone, or something, to jump out of the trees at him anytime. There was a sense of wariness about him at all times.

Today, Jansen was dressed in faded jeans and a grey hooded sweatshirt with the word *Chiefs* stencilled across the chest in navy blue block letters. On his feet, he wore battered old hiking boots and a dark blue ball cap shaded his eyes from the afternoon sun. Heidi's breath caught at the sight of the man as he stepped into the clearing. His ruggedness stirred animalistic instincts buried deep inside. Heidi felt a bead of moisture trickle down between her breasts that had little to do with the day's temperature or activities.

"Hello there!" called Jansen as he got closer. He leaned up against the truck and looked over the edge of the truck bed at the boxes piled inside.

"Hi," Heidi answered back. She closed the tailgate with a loud bang and dusted her hands off on her jeans. "What brings you out here this afternoon?'

Jansen's eyes darkened as he watched Heidi rub her hands along her thighs. She was wearing a pair of jeans that hugged each delicious curve like a race car on a fast track and a fitted top the colour of pure cream. When she leaned against the back of the truck, a band of smooth, tanned skin was exposed between the hem of her shirt and the waistband of her jeans. A belly button peeked out just above her jeans. Jansen's mouth went dry when he caught sight of a tiny diamond winking in the sun. Heidi had a belly ring! The ring hinted at a wildness that Jansen was suddenly very eager to explore further.

For a brief minute, Jansen forgot everything. Where he was. What he was doing. Who he was even. All he could focus on was the ring in Heidi's navel.

A hand waving in front of his face brought Jansen back to earth. "Earth to Jansen. Earth to Jansen. Anyone home?"

Jansen shook himself, trying to clear all thoughts of Heidi's belly button ring from his mind. "Uh, sorry. Just had a brain lapse there for a moment. Recurring injury that hits me when I least expect it. Gladys mentioned that you were moving some of your stuff into storage today so I thought I would swing by to see if you needed any help. As a way of saying thank you for being my tour guide the last couple of days."

"Well," Heidi said. She stepped back and looked Jansen up and down, as if sizing him up. "I'm not one to turn down free help. Especially when it comes from such a strong looking man as yourself. I think you could handle a box or two."

"I have been known to handle my fair share of boxes." Jansen stood up a little straighter and posed for Heidi to give her a better look at what he had to offer. "I was champion box-mover in my younger days. Would have went all-state if I hadn't sprained my index finger during the last move of the season."

Heidi could not help but laugh at Jansen's act. And she could not help but admire the strong masculine body in front of her. The worn denim stretched across thick thighs and along lean calves. Even though the bulky sweater hid Jansen's torso from view, Heidi knew that it covered a sculpted chest and bulging biceps. She suddenly wanted to see if his butt was really as tight as it looked.

"Well. How about I make you a deal," Heidi said. She was surprised that her voice sounded so normal when she felt anything but. "I've got two loads of boxes to move. Including this one that I've already got in the truck. If you help me take everything to storage, I'll treat you to a banana split at The General Store."

"Make it a double fudge brownie sundae and you've got yourself a deal."

Heidi chuckled. "A little bit of a chocolate addict are we now?"

"My one weakness. Come on. Let's get a move on." Jansen opened the passenger side door and climbed in. "I hear a sundae calling my name."

Heidi climbed in beside Jansen and started the truck. She liked that Jansen had not assumed that he would be the one to drive like most men would. Instead, he had settled in the passenger seat, rolled down the window to let in the gentle breeze, and prepared to check out the neighbourhood on the way to her grandfather's house.

Heidi could not believe how easy Jansen fit into her life. It was almost as if he had been customed made for her.

Jansen looked across the table at Heidi as she dug into the mound of ice cream and whipped topping in front of her. He watched as she wrapped her lips around the spoon and then slowly pulled it back out of her mouth. He barely managed to stifle a groan.

"Oops. You missed some. Here, let me get it for you." Jansen reached across the table and wiped a dollop of whipped cream off the end of Heidi's nose. He drew his hand back but Heidi stopped him before it got too far away.

Impulsively, Heidi's tongue darted out and drew the whipped cream-covered finger into her mouth. Her tongue circled around Jansen's finger, cleaning it of all traces of the dessert.

This time Jansen was unable to stop the groan from escaping. Heidi's tongue wrapped around his finger sent shivers down his back. He could feel his body starting to overheat.

Heidi suddenly realised what she was doing. She quickly let go of Jansen's hand and stared down at her melting ice cream. She could feel her cheeks burning. "I...I'm sorry," Heidi stuttered. "I don't know why I did that."

Jansen gulped for air. He tried to nonchalantly brush off the incident. "We wouldn't want to let any of this delicious dessert go to waste. You can't get real whipping cream like this at too many places anymore."

Heidi breathed a quiet sigh of relief. She followed Jansen's lead and tried to act as if nothing had just happened. "The whipping cream is a tradition here at The General Store. It's a family recipe that has been passed down from generation to generation. Ned's the fifth Horton to be serving the family's famous whipping cream."

"That's amazing." Jansen helped up a heaping spoon of whipped cream and studied it closely. "I can't believe that I'm eating something with so much history and tradition."

"There are lots of stories like that in town here. Businesses have been passed down from one generation to the next. It's part of what makes this town so charming and quaint."

"It must be pretty interesting to be part of so much history."

"Some days. But sometimes it can be a little stifling." Heidi stirred together the syrup and melted ice cream left in her bowl. She could not make herself look Jansen in the eye. She could not stand to see the questions in them. Questions that would be quickly replaced with pity as she gave the answers.

"I've always dreamed of owning a hardware store in a little town something like Hadey's Cove," Jansen said. There was a wistful note in his voice as he talked about his dream. "An old fashioned store with a little bit of everything. A place where people can catch up with their neighbours while picking up a bag of nails. A place where a young boy can buy his first hammer and learn how to pound a nail."

"It sounds like you have it all planned out."

Jansen shook his head, a sad look flitting across his face. He pushed the empty sundae dish away and leaned his elbows on the table. "Not really. All I have is a far-fetched dream with no way of making it a reality."

Heidi sensed that this was a touchy subject. One that Jansen was not eager to pursue. She tried to steer the conversation to a safer, less intense area. "What do you do for a living now? From breakfast the other day, I got the impression that you do some kind of consulting work or something."

"Gord and I run a small security business," Jansen answered. Although it was a well practiced, and often used, story, he felt a little uncomfortable telling it to Heidi. He wanted to tell her the truth but it was too soon. And too complicated. He had to make sure that she would be able to handle everything when he did tell her the complete truth. For now, he would have to keep his real occupation a secret. "We help companies set up their security systems. And the occasional wealthy and famous person."

"That sounds interesting. I bet you've met all kinds of neat people."

"There have definitely been a wide range of clients go through our office. But my favourite part of the job is getting to play with all the latest high tech gadgets and gizmos."

Heidi laughed. "Typical male."

"What?" Jansen feigned a hurt look.

"There are only two things that men are interested in. And one of them is the latest high-tech toys."

"And what, may I ask, is the other one?" Jansen leaned across the table and pinned Heidi with an intense look. "Come on now. Spill the beans. What is the only other thing that men are interested in?"

"Umm..." Heidi blushed as she realised the huge hole that she had just stepped into. She glanced around furtively, trying to find another answer. Her gaze settled on the empty bowls on the table between them. "Food! The other thing is food!"

Jansen chuckled. He knew that food was not what Heidi had been originally thinking about. "Nice save. But I don't think that that was what you were first meaning."

"Of course it was!" Heidi protested. She tried to hold a straight face but one look at Jansen had her chuckling behind her hand. "As much as I would like to continue this discussion on male interests, or lack there of, I probably should get back home and back to straightening up my place."

"Okay. We can continue this discussion another day. I'm sure that I'll have no trouble remembering where we left off."

"I bet," Heidi mumbled as she stood up and led Jansen out of The General Store. "Come on, buddy. Let's go. I'll give you a ride back to the inn."

Chapter Eleven

It was a Friday night tradition at Water's Edge Inn: a huge bonfire, complete with wieners and marshmallows, on the beach. All the guests, and many of the townspeople, came out to roast a few marshmallows, tell a few ghost stories, and sing a few songs.

Jansen was not completely sure why he had let himself be dragged out to the bonfire. He tended to shy away from large, rowdy gatherings like this, preferring more intimate and quiet settings to share company in. But the quivering lip and teary eyes of the young blonde woman, currently with her arm linked through his, had broken through his resolve, even though it had been an obviously over-practised routine. In the end, he thought it might be safer to take her to a public place. There would be less chance of her trying to initiate something he really was not interested in. Part of the reason that he agreed to go anywhere was to take his mind off Heidi. She had been taking up too many of his thoughts lately and he was afraid of falling in too deep. Jansen thought this date might prove to be a good diversion.

"I just love ghost stories," purred the woman beside Jansen. She ran a blood red manicured fingernail the length of Jansen's arm. "Especially when I have someone so strong and gallant to protect me. They scare me so much but I just can't help myself."

"I don't think you're going to have to worry too much about that tonight, Becky," Jansen replied. He glanced around, taking in the people milling between the tables of food and roaring bonfires. "By the amount of kids running around here, I don't think the stories will get too graphic or detailed. Probably just a few summer camp urban legends and nothing more. Would you like to roast a hot dog or marshmallow?"

"Ummm...I love roasted marshmallows but I am terrible at roasting them. I almost always burn them." Becky brushed up against Jansen, pressing the length of her body along his. She batted her extended, black lashes in an overly obvious attempt at flirting. "Would you be a dear and toast one for me?"

"Sure," Jansen mumbled. He was really starting to regret agreeing to accompany Becky to the bonfire. It was shaping up to be a long night of fighting her off. As soon as he could, he was going to beg off for the night and head back to his room for some peace.

Jansen led her over to a long table laden with bags of large, fluffy marshmallows and long, double twined roasting sticks. He picked up a stick recently abandoned by a fellow guest and pierced two marshmallows. Finding a spot around the fire, Jansen slowly turned the marshmallows around and around over a bed of red coals. He concentrated on cooking the marshmallows to a perfect golden brown. Becky hovered behind him, never letting Jansen get too far away.

When the marshmallows were roasted to perfection, Jansen moved from his spot by the fire to allow someone else access to it. He gently blew on the gooey, brown globs on the end of the stick before gingerly pulling one off. Instead of taking the marshmallow from his fingers, Becky brought Jansen's hand up to her mouth. She nibbled delicately at the sticky mess before pulling it into her mouth with a slow flick of her tongue. After she had finished, she wrapped her lips around each of Jansen's fingers to remove any lingering traces of the sticky sugar. She tried to portray with her every action how the night might end if Jansen was interested.

Heidi stood by the fire, watching the orange and red flames dance and swirl in time to their own inner music. Its heat caressed her and soothed away her troubles. A bonfire had always calmed Heidi when she was young. She would sit for hours just watching the flames as they licked at the logs. Her father had started the Friday night bonfire when she was just a young girl. She was happy to see that her mother had decided to carry on the tradition and to include others in it.

"I think I managed to cook the wieners without burning them too much," said a voice beside Heidi. The man held the two wieners up for Heidi's inspection. "If you would like, I could go get us a couple of buns and bring them back here."

Heidi shook herself out of her reverie. She turned her attention back to her guest with a smile. "They look great. That would be nice. Thank you, David. I love sitting by the fire and would hate to lose such good seats."

"I'll be right back then. Is there anything in particular that you would like on your hot dog?"

"Just the usual is fine. A little ketchup, mustard, and relish," answered Heidi. She watched as David walked away towards the hot dog table. Heidi had just met David this morning at breakfast. He was new to the inn, having just arrived late the previous night. They had started a conversation over the scrambled eggs and carried it on over minestrone soup and chicken salad wraps at lunch. David felt like a comfortable old friend. Someone Heidi could talk to without worrying about deeper, underlying feelings and mixed signals. She had suggested attending the bonfire that night as a way of him getting to know more people at the inn and from town. David had jumped at the invitation. He had admitted to being somewhat on the shy side, a recluse according to his sisters.

Heidi watched as people moved around the fire, cooking wieners or roasting marshmallows. A flicker of light dancing off a dark head out of the corner of her eye caught her attention. Heidi turned to take a closer look at what attracted her. She took a sharp intake of breath when she recognised the person whom the hair belonged to. Jansen. She watched as he stood and moved away from the fire. A curvy young blonde dressed in the latest body-bearing fashion slid to his side before he could get too far away. Heidi could not tear her eyes away as the woman licked the marshmallow from Jansen's fingers. Tendrils of emotion curled around Heidi's heart as she took in the display. The woman exuded sexuality with her every move. Her actions were intent on securing one outcome—Jansen in her bed by night's end.

"Here you are my darling," David said, breaking Heidi's concentration. She turned away from the scene to reach up and accept the napkin-wrapped hot dog that David was holding out to her. "One fire roasted hot dog á la David. Sorry it took me so long but the line up for buns is a long one. And then everyone wanted to stop and talk. I've never met so many friendly people in one place."

"Hadey's Cove is known for it's warm hospitality and friendliness. It can be a little frustrating when you want to get something done but it is nice to know that so many people care."

"It is quite a difference compared to the city. I've lived in the same townhouse for ten years and still don't know my neighbours." David shook his head sadly. He took a large bite of his hot dog, squirting mustard out the side and onto the corner of his mouth. He tried to dab at the offending yellow liquid but only managed to spread it further across his cheek.

Heidi laughed at David's vain attempts to clean his face. She reached over with her napkin and swatted David's hand out of the way so she could wipe away the mess. "Here, let me help you. You're only making things worse."

"Ahh...thank you. My own lady knight to rescue a commoner in distress," David said. He gently took the hand that Heidi held the mustard-stained napkin in and placed a light kiss along her knuckles. His actions caused Heidi to chuckle even more.

"Oh, David. You can really be too much," Heidi giggled. "A little over the top but very enjoyable all the same."

"I do aim to entertain."

"And that you can do quite well." Heidi crumbled up the napkin that had been around her hot dog and threw it onto the fire. She watched as the fire licked at it before engulfing it completely in flames. "I never got to ask you this morning why you were staying at Water's Edge Inn. You came alone and don't seem to know anyone here or in the area. What drew you to this little place in the middle of no where?"

"I'm looking for a new place to spark my inner creativity. I'm a writer by trade," explained David. His napkin followed Heidi's into the fire and was soon to meet the same fate. "And am trying to work on my next novel. But the city doesn't hold any inspiration anymore. I'm looking for a new place to be my muse. My editor has stayed here a couple of times in the past and suggested that I try it. He said something about it being quaint and idyllic. So here I am."

"What kind of novels do you write? Anything that I might know?" asked Heidi. David's story intrigued her. She had started thinking more and more writing a children's book but was unsure about how to start. Maybe David would be able to give her a few pointers.

"Mostly historical. Kings and queens and knights and damsels in distress and such. I'm a big medieval times buff. Ask me anything about that era and I can tell you." David rubbed the toe of his worn sneaker in the dirt. He did not like to brag about his successes as an author. Usually he kept what he did for a living private. He let his editor and publicist promote his books. But something about Heidi put him at ease and encouraged him to spill his innermost thoughts. Maybe it was the kindred spirit that he sensed in her. "As for my popularity, I guess that depends on whether or not you like the genre that I write for. I've had a few books on New York's best sellers list in the past. But I don't write for fame and fortune. I write because I like to spin stories. The fact that I can do it for a living, and live comfortably doing it, is just a bonus. I would probably write whether I sold anything or not."

Heidi leaned into David's shoulder in a gesture of friendly jest. "Such a noble man you are. Writing to entertain the masses at your own expense."

David chuckled at Heidi's ribbing. The beginnings of a

story idea were beginning to trickle through his subconscious. Maybe he had found the muse that he was looking for. "Somebody has to make the sacrifice. And if it must be me, I will do so graciously."

Heidi laughed at David's act of chivalry. It felt good to laugh, to have something meaningless to laugh about. Heidi felt the stress of the last few days of unpacking wash away as the laughter bubbled from deep inside. It had been a good idea to come tonight. A bonfire had always held some magic within its flames that made things better. Tonight it did not let her down. With Jansen, Heidi always felt on edge, battling the riot of emotions that he invoked in her. But David made Heidi feel comfortable and relaxed. She was not consumed with any other emotion than that of friendship.

As Becky continued to snuggle up to Jansen, never letting him get more than an arm's length away, Jansen felt himself comparing her more and more to Heidi. Heidi was almost Becky's polar opposite, never letting him get more than an arm's length near her. But Heidi intrigued him. She did not try to attract male attention with well-practised flirtation. Instead, her demeanour was more aloof and almost stand-offish. That aloofness was what drew Jansen to her. He wanted to delve into her psyche to find out what made her tick, what made her laugh, and what made her sad. Heidi was not transparent, like Becky, but was a mysterious creature with layers upon layers waiting to be unravelled.

Jansen would have normally been steered more to woman like Becky. They were easy to understand and easy to walk away from. He was not challenged by them, a nice refresher when his work required so much of his concentration. And in his mind, women like Becky were not settling-down material. Heidi was. That thought scared Jansen more than he cared to admit. And more than he could handle right now.

Tension settled between Jansen's shoulders. He tried to stretch some of the stiffness out but to no avail. The knot was a stubborn one.

Becky saw Jansen trying to roll his shoulders. She ran a hand up along his spine with feather-light pressure. "Is something the matter, hon?" she asked.

Jansen shook his head in response. "No. My back's just a little tight. I must have pulled something the other day when I was helping a friend move."

"Well, you are in luck then. I am famous for my back rubs. These hands can undo even the most stubborn muscles." Becky gently pushed Jansen down onto a log bench before he could protest. She used her fingers to knead and rub the muscles between Jansen's shoulder blades. With even pressure, she worked the tension out of his back.

As Becky worked on his back, Jansen watched the people around him enjoying the bonfire. Someone caught his eye through the dancing flames. He watched as the woman he was desperately trying to forget snuggle up to another man. He was tall and fair with a well-honed body. They were laughing and joking together. Everything looked very cosy. Almost too cosy. The tension returned to set up residence between Jansen's shoulders once again.

Jansen was not used to feeling this way about another person. He had only ever allowed himself to love his best friend Gord. Gord had always been there no matter what; everyone else in his life had deserted him when the going got tough. But there was something about Heidi that he could not shake. She was wheedling her way past all his defences without even trying. She had gotten under his skin whether she wanted to or not. Jansen was not ready to put a name to the deep emotion filling his heart right now. Instead, he focused on the emotion that was taking over his conscious thoughts right now. Jealousy.

No other time in his life could Jansen remember feeling this jealous, this quickly. It bubbled up to consume him in his blindness. He was beginning to see how crimes could be committed in a fit of jealousy. Right now, he had the strongest urge to go over and teach the stranger a thing or two about manners. Jansen had never been this jealous about anything in his life. He had felt the odd twinge of the emotion when someone at work got an assignment or promotion that he had been wanting, but it had never been this intense. What was he to do about it? How was he to control it? What does a person do when he is so filled with jealousy he wants to do bodily harm?

Heidi deserved to be happy. And she had every right to go out with anyone that she chose to. There was nothing formal about Heidi and Jansen's relationship. They were merely new friends spending time together getting to know each other. If attending a bonfire with the attractive stranger helped Heidi to heal from the past, then Jansen should be happy. He should encourage it more. Heidi needed to get on with her life in her own way. Jansen was not going to be around here forever. Heidi would need to find someone else to help her get through the lonely days and nights with.

All these arguments coursed through Jansen's head but they did little to ease the feelings running riot through his body. He knew that Heidi's happiness came first over anything else and that however she started the healing process was her decision. None of this helped to control his jealousy though. Jansen had wanted to be the one to bring Heidi out of the past and give her something to live for again. Jansen wanted to be the one to take Heidi's hand and pull her back into the present and lead her into the future.

These thoughts startled Jansen. He shook his head slightly to clear them from his mind. He could not have these strong feelings for Heidi. There was no room for them in his line of work. And he had not exactly come to Hadey's Cove and to Heidi with the innocent of intentions. He had come here for a reason. When, or if, Heidi found out the complete truth about him, she would probably never want to see him again anyway. He had to nip these feelings in the bud before they got too carried away and he did something he would regret.

A soft breath of air against his ear brought Jansen out of his thoughts. Becky leaned over and whispered in Jansen's ear, "You know, if you play your cards right, I could give you a full body massage. I also specialise in areas a little lower on the body, if you get my drift. I leave no one unsatisfied."

The proposition was tempting for a split second. Jansen could use Becky to help him try and forget about the captivating woman sitting across the fire from him. He could bury himself in another's arms to hide from the truth trying to sneak up on him. He could use someone else to escape from the feelings he did not want to admit were there. But Jansen was not that kind of man. He was not a user. If Jansen spent the night with a woman, it was because there was a connection there. Gord was the one to sleep around, not Jansen.

Jansen sighed. Things had gotten so complicated so quickly. This was supposed to be a vacation of sorts. First Jansen was going to excuse himself from a situation he should never had gotten himself into and then he was going to go back to his room alone and try to put everything back into perspective. "Thanks for the massage, Becky. But that's were it's gotta end. I'm not into one night stands and this would be nothing more than that. I think it's best if I just go now before things go any further. Thank you for inviting me to the bonfire. I had a good time. Maybe we can do lunch or something at the inn."

Jansen walked away before Becky could protest. He did not like leaving her alone but somehow he knew that Becky would not stay alone for long. She was not the kind of girl to be without a man on her arm for long. Jansen threaded his way through the crowd of revellers standing around the bonfires and headed back towards the inn. It had been a long night and he was eager for it to end.

Heidi had been watching Jansen and his date out of the corner of her eye while she enjoyed a few roasted marshmallows with David. She watched as the leggy blonde rubbed Jansen's broad back. In Heidi's mind, the blonde bimbo's head replaced the marshmallow at the end of the roasting stick. She dipped the gooey mound further into the flames until it caught on fire. Satisfaction filled her as she watched the marshmallow smoulder and turn black.

"I have never understood the appeal of eating charred marshmallow," stated David, breaking into Heidi's thoughts. He pulled a perfectly browned marshmallow from the end of his stick and popped it into his mouth. "Charred steak or salmon, yes. But not marshmallows. Burnt sugar just doesn't sound very appetising to me."

Heidi knocked the blackened mess into the coals and set the roasting stick on the ground beside her. She had had enough of roasting for now. The desire to start something, or more specifically someone, on fire startled her. The emotions flooding through Heidi were so intense that she almost wanted to inflict bodily harm on someone. It was so unlike her to react this strongly to anything that she did not know how to handle it. She decided to try to push the riot of emotions down and deal with them later. Maybe if she was removed from the situation, she would be a little more level-headed and be able to figure out why she was really being so irrational.

"I usually don't like my marshmallows roasted too much either," agreed Heidi. She turned slightly, trying to put Jansen and his date out of her line of sight. Out of sight out of mind. "Sometimes, though, I just like to see how black I can get the marshmallow before it falls off. It's the pyromaniac in me I guess."

David chuckled. The vibes emitting from Heidi were causing his creative gears to go into overdrive. Even though he was anxious to return to his room and get his thoughts down on paper, he remained seated beside Heidi and tried to make conversation. He did not want to run out on her, especially after she had invited him to this bonfire. And he was enjoying her company. If he ran away now, he may insult and alienate her. That was not a good thing to do with a muse.

A comfortable silence settled between Heidi and David as they each lost themselves in their thoughts. David played out scenes from his next great novel in his head. Heidi tried to distract herself from the feelings of jealousy that tried to invade her mind. There was no way that she wished to be the blonde woman draped on Jansen's arm. She was happy being alone. Over and over, she tried to convince herself of this.

After enjoying a brief fireworks display in each other's company, David and Heidi agreed it was time to call it a night. David returned to his room and his computer where he worked into the wee hours of the morning. Heidi returned to her cottage and her memories where she tried to chase all thoughts of a tall, dark stranger from her dreams.

Chapter Twelve

A soft breeze rippled over the surface of the lake, sending tiny waves crashing against the wooden rowboat bobbing lazily in the water. Heidi leaned back and turned her face up to the warming rays of the sun. A lone seagull called out to the sky as it soared overhead.

Jansen watched as Heidi relaxed at the other end of the boat. A few strands of hair had come loose from her braid and curled softly around her face. His eyes traced the outline of her lean frame, taking in the pale yellow tank top and cut-off shorts that hinted at the sweetness beneath. He could just see a trace of creamy white breasts over the edge of the tank top. With each deep breath she took, it looked as if her breasts would break free of the restraining material.

Jansen yearned to take a breast in his hand, to test its weight, to test its fit in his palm. He wanted to massage the nipple into a hard point. He wanted to wrap his lips around it and tease it with his tongue.

Heidi shifted slightly to stretch her legs out into a more comfortable position. Jansen inhaled sharply at the sight of the long tanned legs. The short shorts could not hide her muscular thighs. Jansen imagined running his tongue along the inside of each thigh before tasting the sweetness that lay between. His blood boiled with the overwhelming need to bury himself between Heidi's legs. Jansen could feel his arousal straining against his shorts as his mind filled with erotic images of Heidi's naked body.

Heidi was unaware of the effect that she was having on Jansen. She was enjoying the peace, the gentle movement of the water, the warm afternoon sun. It had been a good idea to accept Jansen's invitation to go fishing, even though they had not even had a nibble yet. Being out on the lake, rocking gently on the waves, had relaxed Heidi more than she had been in a long time. Life was so much simpler when nothing but calm water and blue sky surrounded a person.

"I wish I could stay out here forever," sighed Heidi. She dragged a hand lazily through the cool water.

"It is beautiful out here," Jansen agreed. He shifted so that he was looking out across the wide expanse of the water instead of at Heidi. He tried to think of something boring and mundane like his grocery list to erase the heated thoughts from his mind. He tried to take a few deep breaths to slow his throbbing pulse.

"When I was young, I used to spend hours out on the lake just like this," said Heidi. Her eyes had a far away look in them as she remembered long ago days. "It was one of my favourite places when the people started coming. The only place I could ever be really alone. And when I was young and mad at the world, I would come out here and plot my revenge.

"I could never stay mad out here long, though. It was as if the waves would wash everything away and just leave the bare facts. The problem never seemed as big or as earth-shattering after a few hours of bobbing around out here."

Jansen glanced over at Heidi during her retrospect. The utter peacefulness that enveloped her struck a cord deep within him. He envied her for it. Never once had he been able to look back on his life and feel so content. There was always too much baggage, too much turmoil to taint the good memories.

"I needed a place like this when I was young," said Jansen quietly. "Maybe then I wouldn't have gotten into so much trouble."

"A little trouble maker were you?" teased Heidi, a grin lighting up her face. Her eyes gleamed with a hint of mischief.

"More like rebelling against society." Jansen shrugged his shoulders. He kept his eyes fixed on some faraway spot on the other side of the lake. He did not want Heidi to see the pain and sorrow that he knew were in his eyes. They were always there whenever he thought of his childhood.

"I hardly know anything about you but you seem to know everything about me. Tell me something about yourself," Heidi prodded. She sat up and wrapped her arms around her legs. She studied Jansen with interest, trying to imagine what he would have been like as a young boy. "Where did you grow up? What were your parents like?"

"There's not much to tell." Jansen said. A muscle twitched along his jaw. He was battling his emotions, trying to keep the hurt and anger at bay. "I grew up on the wrong side of the proverbial tracks. My father was an alcoholic who liked to beat on my mom. He beat her to death when I was fourteen and I was put into a state foster home for unwanted kids."

"I'm so sorry, Jansen," Heidi whispered. She reached over and laid a hand gently on his arm.

At her touch, Jansen turned. He looked into eyes filled with pain and pity. It was the pity that bothered him the most. Though his childhood had hardened him early, he did not regret the way things had turned out in the end. There had been too many good people along the way who had tried to help him. And he may not have ended up where he was today if his childhood had been different.

"Oh, it wasn't always that bad," Jansen said quickly. He tried to call up some good memories to lighten some of the tension. "I have some good memories of friends and neighbours. Of happy times. I met my partner in the foster home and we have been inseparable ever since. Things have turned out pretty good considering how it started."

Jansen gave Heidi a big smile, a smile that did not quite clear the dark clouds from his eyes, to show her that everything was okay. She moved back to her end of the boat and puzzled over the change in Jansen's attitude. There was more to the story than he let on. More to the pain and anguish he was trying to hide. Even though he was smiling, she could tell that it was forced. She had forced enough smiles in the past couple of years to know when a smile was not genuine.

"Since the fish aren't biting today, why don't we head back to the shore and see if there is any other trouble that we can get ourselves into," suggested Jansen.

Heidi sensed that Jansen had had enough of talking about his past. She understood how he felt. More often than not lately, she wished people would leave the past alone and let her focus on the present. It was hard enough to deal with the present lately, never mind adding in things that had already happened. She said, "Sure. I think I heard some rumblings about a beach volleyball game this morning at breakfast. Could be entertaining with some of the guests staying here."

"Can you imagine ole Art in a pair of trunks diving after the ball?"

Heidi grimaced as a picture of Art, wearing nothing but shorts with his expansive white belly hanging over the waistband and skinny chicken legs sticking out, flashed through her mind. "I would rather not, thank you very much."

Jansen and Heidi bantered lightly back and forth as they pulled in their empty lines, packed up their gear, and headed back to shore. The mood in the boat lightened as the water washed off its sides.

The volleyball game was just starting as Heidi and Jansen trudged back up the sandy beach to the net that had been strung up in one corner of the sand. The adults had challenged their younger counterparts to a best of three match, each game to fifteen points. In a concession to their greater skill level and athleticism as well as their youth, the teenagers had graciously suggested that the adults could play with as many people on the court at one time as they wanted. They would only play with four people and substitute after every serve.

Heidi spread her towel out beside the few adults who had nominated themselves as cheerleaders. The elderly lady next to her passed over a colourful paper pompom to wave whenever the adults scored a point. Heidi chuckled at the lady's enthusiasm as she danced and cheered for their team. She only hoped that she would have half of her energy when she was the same age.

Jansen was pulled into the match before he could come up with a suitable argument for staying on the sidelines beside Heidi. The older men saw a fit younger body and latched onto it like barnacles to the bottom of a ship. Every advantage they could get was a bonus.

The adults fought gamely against the teenagers. They learned fast, though, that having six or seven players on the court at one time was not necessarily a good thing. The crowd erupted in laughter and cat calls as Ed, the rail-thin shoe salesman, was ploughed over by a much more generously proportioned Clarence as he dove after the ball. Body parts clashed in attempts to keep the ball in the air and return it back over the net in only three hits.

The first game ended in a trouncing by the teenagers, but after a team huddle, the adults regrouped and beat the teenagers in a squeaker in the second game. It all came down to the final game—a do-or-die contest for all the marbles.

Heidi found herself caught up in the excitement of the match. The enthusiasm of the people around her was infectious. By the final game, she had joined up with four other ladies to form an impromptu cheerleading squad. They jumped and kicked and cheered to chants they remembered from high school and to ones they made up as they went along.

Jansen watched Heidi from the corner of his eye as she pranced around in the sand. His heart pounded in his chest as he took in her lithe body twisting and twirling. Her cheeks were flushed a rosy colour and her eyes sparkled with merriment. They looked alive after being dead for so long. At the end of one chant, Heidi performed a series of cartwheels and flips, finishing with the splits. Jansen's breath caught in his throat as he pictured Heidi in bed using that flexibility to send him to heaven and back.

Heidi was also watching Jansen out of the corner of her eye as he tried to concentrate on the volleyball game. She admired the play of muscles across his shoulders as he bumped the ball into the air. He had washboard abs that would be the envy of any male. There was a smattering of dark hair across his chest that tapered down to a vee just above his swim trunks. His trunks hung low on his hips, caressing his buttocks like a lover. Thick, tanned legs extended out of the bottom, legs that could crush a person if wrapped around them. A sheen of sweat glistened on Jansen's skin. Heidi could almost taste the saltiness on her tongue. She ached to run her tongue along the ridges of his muscles, across that hard chest. She longed to take a dark nipple in her mouth and coax it into hardness.

Jansen leaped into the air with a powerful thrust of his legs, smashing the ball across the air and ending the game. The adults won. They beat the teenagers two games to one. Everyone rushed onto the court to congratulate the teams on an excellent, and very entertaining, match. Jansen was soon engulfed in a crowd of well-wishers slapping him on the back and pumping his hand for a job well done. Heidi hung back at the edges of the crowd, suddenly unsure of herself. Jansen searched the crowd trying to find her. Their eyes met over the heads of the people around them. The air crackled between them. They drowned in each other's eyes, both dark with pent-up emotions yearning to be shared.

"Thank you for such an enjoyable day," said Jansen. He and Heidi were walking back to her tiny cottage tucked in the trees. A full, silver moon lit the way. "I don't think I've laughed so much in a long time."

"Me neither," agreed Heidi. She absently ruffled the pompoms that she had used to cheer the adults to victory. It had been a long time since the past had not plagued Heidi's every action. She had been able to put aside the sadness in her heart for a few hours and truly enjoy herself. "That volleyball game was better than I thought."

"I'm just glad that Art declined to join. Things might have turned scary then. Especially for poor Ed. He took a few rough shots out there. I hate to think what might have happened if it had been Art instead of Clarence who had run over Ed. We might have lost Ed in all that belly fat." Jansen shuddered at the mental picture that his mind had formed.

Heidi playfully slapped Jansen on the shoulder in Art's defence. She lightly admonished him, "You shouldn't be so hard on the guy. He is a very nice person."

"I know. I know. And I'm sure that he can't help being the way that he is."

Jansen rubbed at his shoulder, pretending that Heidi's light tap had hurt more than it actually did, in attempt to illicit some sympathy.

Suddenly, Heidi stopped walking. She laid a hand on Jansen's arm to stop him and pressed a finger to his lips when he started to ask what was wrong. Then she pointed to where two young fox cubs were rolling among the ferns. They stood watching the pups playing, oblivious to the humans standing just a few feet away.

Jansen leaned down and whispered in Heidi's ear, "Maybe we should leave before Momma comes and sees us."

Heidi simply nodded. The warm breath brushing the back of her neck sent waves of tingles crashing through her body. She stood frozen as the sensations over took her senses.

Jansen took Heidi's hand and gently pulled her away from the cubs. He led the way back to the cottage. Heidi lost focus on where they were going. All she could concentrate on was the feel of her hand in Jansen's. It was strong and worked roughened. His long fingers wrapped around her hand in a secure, yet gentle, grip. Heidi knew she should take her hand back, but for some reason, could not make her traitorous limb do her bidding.

Jansen led Heidi into the middle of her fragrant garden. The flowers bobbed gently in the evening breeze. Overhead, millions of twinkling stars studded the velvet sky. Jansen stopped among the dahlias and turned to face Heidi. He pulled her gently to him.

Heidi looked up at Jansen, slightly dazed. The moonlight glinted off the top of his head and surrounded him in a blanket of silver light. She reached up and brushed a stray lock of hair from Jansen's eye.

Jansen groaned softly. He turned his head slightly and pressed a kiss to the palm of Heidi's hand. It tasted salty beneath his lips. Slowly, Jansen traced gentle kisses across her palm. He could feel her pulse quicken as his lips brushed against the inside of her wrist.

Jansen pulled back a little and looked down at Heidi. Her tongue flicked across her dry lips, leaving a wet sheen behind. Her eyes, beneath heavy lids, were dark with desire. Jansen leaned down and gently pressed his lips to hers. She gasped slightly before wrapping her arms around his neck and pulling him closer to her. Jansen tilted his head and deepened the kiss in response.

Slowly, Jansen moved his hands down Heidi's arms to the small of her back. At the same time, his tongue begged to enter Heidi's mouth. She parted her lips slightly. It was all the invitation Jansen needed. He tenderly probed the sweetness, encouraging Heidi to open up fully for him. While his tongue coaxed Heidi's to do some exploring of her own, Jansen's hands moved down to cup Heidi's bottom. He lifted her against him, pressing her into his arousal.

Heidi gasped when she felt the hardness between her thighs. Reality began to seep into her brain and the fog cleared. Panic set in. She pushed against Jansen's chest, trying to free herself.

Jansen looked down at Heidi and became alarmed. Fear had replaced the passion in her eyes. He quickly released Heidi and stepped back.

"Oh God, Heidi. I'm sorry. I should never have done that," apologised Jansen. He groaned inwardly at his stupidity and lack of constraint. He knew that Heidi was in a fragile emotional state right now. Once again, he had let his hormones get the better of him. Like some horny teenager. He just could not seem to help himself though, whenever he was around her. And he could not force himself to stay away.

"I...I have to go," Heidi mumbled. Before Jansen could say anything, she turned and fled to the safety of her cottage.

Jansen cursed loudly to the moon overhead. He briefly considered going after Heidi to make sure she was alright but knew that it would not be a good idea. He could not trust himself to keep his hands off her right now. Instead, he headed back to the main house and a long, cold shower.

Chapter Thirteen

Heidi brushed the sand from the bright beach towel and stretched out on it. She dug through her tote bag in search of the book she had grabbed on impulse at the bus station during one of the layovers on her trip home. It was a sappy romance story where the heroine got into all kinds of trouble and needed the hero to save her. Heidi normally shied away from such fluff but something on the cover had drawn her to the book. Maybe it had been the picture of two people wrapped up in each other, so oblivious to everything around them. Maybe it had been the illusion of escape into someone else's happiness. Heidi could not say for sure but she had not been able to resist buying the book.

Now, Heidi pulled down her sunglasses and prepared to lose herself in the heroine's life. She opened the book to the first page.

"Hello, sunshine," greeted a voice above Heidi. "You really take playing hooky to the limits. Thought you had to do some more unpacking today?"

Heidi squinted up at the dark shadow blocking her sun.

She smiled as she recognized Jansen outlined in a halo of sun. "Hi, Jansen. Just thought I would take a break and catch a few rays. A girl can only resist the call of the sun so much."

"Well, it sure is a beautiful day to be out and about enjoying it. Mind if I join you?" asked Jansen.

"Sure. As long as you don't plan on talking too much. I have a new book I want to start," Heidi said, holding up the book to show Jansen.

Jansen dropped his backpack on the sand and plopped down beside Heidi. He pulled a sketchpad from his bag. "You won't mind if I do a little doodling then?"

"No, go ahead." Heidi glanced over at Jansen as he flipped open his book and picked up a pencil. "What do you doodle?"

"Mostly people," Jansen replied. "I like studying people and trying to draw their hidden characters."

"Got any interesting ones?" Heidi asked curiously. She tried to take a peek at the sketchpad as Jansen flipped to a new page but his shoulder was blocking her line of vision. Without moving and making it obvious that she was snooping, Heidi could not get a clear view of the pad.

"Not yet. It's been awhile since I last picked up a pencil. Thought maybe today was the day to start back at it," Jansen said as he smoothed out a blank sheet of paper. He picked up a pencil and stared at the paper on his knee, waiting for inspiration.

"Well, you definitely picked a good place to watch people." Heidi waved at all the people on the beach. The young adults had started a game of beach volleyball while their kids built sandcastles along the edge of the water. "I think just about everyone is at the beach today. You should be able to find some interesting subjects here."

"That was my thought, too. I looked around at the house but no one seemed to be around. Figured everyone must have heard the same call of the sun and headed down here. So I grabbed my stuff and followed. But I should shut up now and let you read. I could join you only if I was quiet so I should be quiet before you send me away." Jansen pretended to button up his lips, lock them safe and sound, and throw away the key. His antics earned a giggle from Heidi.

"Yeah. And I'm sure you can't draw with me yakking in your ear."

Heidi settled back with her book and Jansen sharpened his pencil in preparation to start drawing something. Heidi tried to read but just could not seem to concentrate. Every nerve was tingling with the nearness of the man beside her. After reading the first paragraph three times, Heidi threw down the book in frustration.

"Book not interesting?" Jansen asked. His eyes never left the page as his hand continued to shade and shape.

"I just can't seem to get into it," answered Heidi. She rolled over on her stomach to watch the game of volleyball going on behind them. "It usually takes me a bit to really get into a book and my mind just doesn't seem to want to concentrate today."

Jansen looked out of the corner of his eye at the long lean body beside him. It was clad in a scanty two-piece. The flowered bottom barely covered a firm set of cheeks and stretched low across the hips. The back of the top consisted of only a thin strap stretching across the middle of the rib cage. Jansen's breath caught in his throat. He longed to run his hands across the creamy white skin of her back. To taste the milkiness of it against his lips. He wanted to slide his body along the length of her's and feel her pressed against him, begging for release.

"How's the drawing coming along?" asked Heidi as she turned back to look at the lake lapping a few feet from her toes.

Jansen shook himself out of his reverie. He felt guilty for having such lusty thoughts about Heidi. She did not need someone jumping all over her right now. She needed a friend. Someone to make her laugh and see that life was worth living again.

He looked down at the sketchpad balanced on his knees. There were a few shaded lines but nothing recognizable. "Apparently not very well," Jansen said, holding up the pad so Heidi could see what he had done so far.

Heidi chuckled at Jansen's sheepish look. "Can't find any inspiration?"

"My mind keeps wandering. I can't seem to concentrate

on the paper in front of me either," Jansen replied as he folded up his sketchbook and stuffed it back in his bag.

"Too busy checking out the hot chicks is it?" teased Heidi. She punched Jansen lightly on the shoulder.

"Just one," Jansen replied.

"Only one?" Heidi raised an eyebrow in Jansen's direction. "I see at least half a dozen young things running around here that have been turning heads all week."

Jansen shrugged his shoulders. "There's only one that's caught my eye."

"Anyone special?" questioned Heidi. She sat up so she could get a better look at Jansen and the women sunning themselves on the beach.

"She's pretty special to me," said Jansen, his voice holding a wistful note. He focused on a distant spot on the lake as he continued, "She's got a quiet strength about her that draws people to her. She's worked her way underneath my skin and I can't seem to get her out no matter how many cold showers I take and how much soap I use."

"She must be a real looker."

"Breathtaking," breathed Jansen. He had taken on a far away look as he thought about the woman. "But it's more than her physical beauty that draws me to her. There is an inner

beauty deep inside her that is just waiting to blossom into a beautiful flower. It's waiting for the dark clouds troubling her soul to part and let the sun in."

Heidi sat watching Jansen for a moment. She did not know how to respond to his description. The conversation had taken on weightier undertones that she did not feel prepared to handle. Emotions that Heidi had so desperately tried to repress came rushing back to the surface. Jealousy bubbled up. Heidi envied the woman who had caught Jansen's attention so completely. For a moment, she wanted to be the one who filled Jansen with such complete rapture. Desperately, Heidi tried to think of something to say that would lighten up the mood again.

Jansen came to Heidi's rescue before she could think of anything. He shook himself from his reverie and turned to Heidi. "Enough of this serious talk. What does a person do in this town at night for a little bit of fun?"

"Depends on what kind of fun you're looking for," teased Heidi. "Good clean fun or something a little more naughty?"

Jansen chuckled. An image of Heidi and some naughty fun flashed through his mind. "I think a little bit of good clean fun is in order for tonight. Something wholesome and innocent."

"Well, Hadey's Cove does have a drive-in that's pretty popular with the younger generation. Or there's a two lane bowling alley."

"Drive-in? Hmmm..." Jansen said. With one eyebrow raised, he looked Heidi up and down. "It's been a while since I've been to a drive-in. Not since I was young lad. And if I recall correctly, there wasn't much good clean fun going on there."

"Yeah, well, Hadey's Cove's a little different," laughed Heidi. A blush stained her cheeks at Jansen's insinuations. "Everybody knows everyone so nobody can get away with any hanky panky at the drive-in without the entire town knowing about it the next day."

"The town sounds like every parent's greatest fantasy. And every teenager's worst nightmare." Jansen leaned back on his elbows and stretched his legs out in front of him. Heidi admired their length and the bronze tone to his skin. No matter how long she stayed out in the sun, she could never achieve that colour. She always burned red like a lobster and then lost all the colour after a few days.

"Pretty much," agreed Heidi. "The citizens of Hadey's Cove are like one big chaperone. Everyone looks out for everyone else. Of course some people more than others."

Jansen sighed, a sad note touching it. His eyes filled with an unsettled look that reminded Heidi of their conversation on the boat just the other day. It made her even more curious about Jansen's past and what was haunting him so much. Jansen said softly, "Must have been great growing up here. Surrounded by people who cared about you."

Heidi shifted away from Jansen to face the lake. She thought for a moment before answering. "It has its good parts and it's bad parts. Good because a person feels secure and safe and well-loved. Bad because you could never do anything without someone knowing about it and telling your parents."

"I wish that I had grown up in a small town like this instead of the city. Might have been a different person when I was young," Jansen said, once again referring to his troubled childhood. "One thing I know for sure is that I would never raise a family in the city."

Heidi glanced over at Jansen. "Do you have a family in the works? A wife? Girlfriend? Kids?"

"Me?" Jansen asked in surprise. He shook his head slowly. "No, I don't have a family. Not married and no girlfriend. Apparently I'm 'too married to my job' to have a serious relationship. Or so the last woman who tried to get me to commit said."

"A workaholic are you?"

"Sort of," admitted Jansen, shrugging his shoulders. "I guess I am just committed to making a difference through my job."

"That was the way that I used to be. But then...then..." Heidi stumbled over the words. She could not tell Jansen about all that she had lost. It was just still too painful to be talking about out loud. "But then I realized that there was more to life than working all the time. So I quit my job and moved back home to try a different avenue."

"Figured out which avenue you're going to turn down?" asked Jansen.

"Not yet. I used to write a little in high school and I can draw half decent so I thought maybe I would try writing a children's book or something."

"Cool! I am sitting on a beach towel with a future world renowned children's author," exclaimed Jansen. He reached into his bag and pulled out his sketchbook. Flipping to a blank page, he thrust the book and a pencil towards Heidi. "Can I have your autograph before you're all rich and famous and won't even talk to me?"

Heidi laughed at Jansen's kidding. It felt good to laugh. To joke around with someone. It's been too long since I did this, Heidi thought. To Jansen, she said, "I don't think you have to worry about not being able to talk to me again. I really don't think I'm going to get rich and famous in my lifetime. Hopefully I'll be able to make enough to feed myself every other day or so."

"I really don't think you'll have anything to worry about. I'm sure you'll be a great at whatever you decide to do," Jansen said, full of confidence for her ability.

Heidi just wished that she could be as sure that everything would work out. She had been doing the same thing for so long now that she was not sure that she would be able to change, to take a new direction, to change her way of thinking. "And how would you know? You've never read anything I've written or seen anything that I've drawn."

"I'm a great judge of character. Made a career out of it in fact. I can just tell that you're great at everything you put your mind to."

"Well, we'll see," said Heidi, unconvinced. "It's just a thought anyway. I might change my mind once I try sitting down with a pen and paper."

"Well, enough serious talk about careers and stuff," said Jansen. He threw the notebook back in his bag and zipped up the opening. "How about a little fun now? Can I interest you in a movie at the drive-in?"

"Oh, I don't know." Heidi idly brushed some sand off her blanket. She could not make herself meet Jansen's eyes filled with hope and warmth. She loved going to the drive-in but part of her was scared to death of being alone in a car with Jansen. She was not sure that she could trust herself to be so close to this man.

"It's not like we would be really alone," said Jansen, trying to convince Heidi to join him. "You said it yourself. The entire town will be there watching our every move."

Heidi could not come up with a suitable argument for that point. She tried one last attempt to convince herself that she should not go. "I really should be unpacking. I've been lazy all day. And those darn unpacking fairies seem to have lost their way here."

"You've got all the time in the world to unpack. It goes better if you work at it little by little. It gives you time to think about where you want to put everything. Come on. You've played hooky this long. Why not a few more hours?" Jansen sat up on his knees and begged Heidi like a puppy dog. He stuck out his bottom lip in a small pout and teared his eyes up.

Heidi sighed in defeat. She knew there was no way she was going to win this argument. And Jansen was right. There would be enough people around to keep her from misbehaving. "Okay. Okay. You win. You've talked me into it. I'll go to the drive-in with you. But you're going to have to buy me the biggest bucket of hot buttered popcorn they have, with extra butter, just to make up for taking me away from my boxes."

"It's a deal." Jansen stood up and held out his hand to help Heidi up. "I'll be by to pick you up in an hour."

"You don't give a girl much time to get ready," chuckled Heidi. She bent down to pick up her towel and bag.

"I don't want to give you any time to change your mind. Now go," said Jansen as he gently pushed Heidi toward her home, "before I walk in on you in the middle of changing."

"I'll be ready," said Heidi. She headed off down the beach but paused long enough to call over her shoulder, "just don't be late yourself."

Heidi settled back against the soft charcoal grey leather seat of Jansen's car. When he had drove up to her door, Heidi had been surprised to see the sunshine yellow sports car. She had pictured Jansen more as the big, tough truck kind of guy. She had expected him to come roaring up in a black four by four diesel with extra-large, well tread tires. Instead, he had arrived in a low slung car that purred like a contented cat.

Jansen had explained that the car was actually his partner's as he held the door open for Heidi. He usually drove a company vehicle so did not have a 'pleasure vehicle', as he called it, of his own. He did not think that he should take the company vehicle on his vacation so he had borrowed Gord's car to tour around in.

"Comfortable?" asked Jansen. "There's not a lot of room in this car to stretch out. Not exactly the best vehicle for going to the drive-in in."

"Depends on what a person's intentions are," said Heidi, a smile spreading across her face. Her eyes glinted in merriment. "If a person was wanting to get a little closer to someone and was on the shy side, this would be the perfect car to do it. Not a whole lot of room to get away from someone."

"Now that's a good point. Maybe this car does have some good points. Feel like getting a little closer?" Jansen cast Heidi an innocent look. His smile was teasing but his eyes smouldered with a deeper emotion.

Heidi could feel the heat spreading over her face. As soon as she said the words, she knew that she had put her foot in her mouth. She did not need to be thinking about snuggling up to anyone. Nor did she need to be putting the suggestion in Jansen's head. She did not want to give him any hints that she might be interested in more.

"I thought I agreed to join you on the condition that nothing would happen," Heidi reminded Jansen. "Remember all the prying eyes around us. We wouldn't want to be tomorrow's coffee shop gossip now would we?"

"Oh, I don't know." Jansen shrugged his shoulders and pretended to debate Heidi's logic in his mind. "The reward would be more than enough to make up for all the pain and embarrassment of the gossip. Especially since no one really knows me around here. I would just be the stranger who stole the virtue of the town's daughter."

Heidi snorted at Jansen's act. He could be as bad as Gord sometimes when it came to flirting. At least Gord did not use an innocent boy act. A person knew that he was flirting. With Jansen, though, you could just never tell for sure how serious he was. And that was harder to resist than Gord's obvious charms.

"Are you sure that Gord is the one to charm all the girls?" asked Heidi. "You seem to have the art of flirtation down pretty good yourself."

Jansen chuckled, "I've had a good teacher."

The drive-in stood at the edge of town, it's wooden screen nestled against the pine trees of the surrounding forest. A line up to get in had already formed by the time Heidi and Jansen arrived. They inched forward with the other cars as the gates opened. When they finally made it through, Jansen picked a spot near the back of the lot, away from the bright lights lighting up the area around the concession stand. He rolled down his window enough to hang the battered speaker on its lip. Old time country songs filled the small interior of the car.

After they had parked, Jansen went to buy the large bucket of buttered popcorn that he had promised Heidi and a couple of cold drinks to wash the salt and butter down. Heidi watched through the windshield as Jansen sauntered towards the concession stand. He had dressed in worn blue jeans that hugged his legs and a loose fitting polo shirt. The clothes hinted at the hard body that was hidden beneath, giving enough of a picture to leave a person begging for more. Heidi's heart fluttered at the thought. Her mind easily conjured by the image of a nearly naked Jansen laughing and joking with the other guests playing volleyball. She groaned softly. This had definitely not been a good idea. The setting was just too cosy for her overactive hormones.

Jansen returned with the popcorn and drinks, passing everything through the window to Heidi so he did not spill anything when getting back into the car. The scent of buttered popcorn quickly filled the interior. Heidi's stomach rumbled loudly in anticipation, causing Jansen to chuckle. The sound washed over Heidi and warmed her from the inside out. She took a sip of the fuzzy soda Jansen had handed her as she tried to gain control of herself again. She tried to make small talk to fill the silence that surrounded them but her brain just would not function properly. All her senses were on overload.

As Heidi struggled to come up with yet another safe topic to talk about, the opening credits flashed on the screen and voices filled the car from the receiver hooked onto the window, spouting the story lines of upcoming movies. Heidi and Jansen turned to the screen to watch the action.

The drive-in was showing a romantic comedy about two people trying to find love and happiness in a small town. Neither Jansen nor Heidi had seen the movie yet, even though it had already been out for six months. Both had said that they had been too busy lately to take time out to go and see a movie.

Heidi tried to concentrate on the characters moving across the screen but she kept seeing herself up there. She became the actress in her mind, struggling to figure out who she was. The actor slowly dissolved into Jansen. During the love scene, she saw Jansen caressing her into a frenzy with his hands, his lips, his tongue. He was the one who dipped his head low to kiss between her thighs. To lap at the sweet nectar of her womanhood.

Heidi could feel herself grow damp as the actor moved back up the actress and pulled her to him. Her pulse quickened as their bodies joined together with one glorious thrust. Heat spread through Heidi in waves. Her breath became shallow and ragged. A faint colouring spread over her cheeks as her body temperature rose.

Jansen glanced quickly over at Heidi as the love scene started to unfold in front of them. By the faint light from the screen, he could see that her eyes had clouded over. The lovemaking was affecting her, exciting her in a way that only a woman who had been long without a man's loving touch could be excited.

Slowly, Jansen reached over and laid his hand across Heidi's thigh. He lazily rubbed circles over the bare skin with this thumb. A soft groan escaped Heidi's lips. She moved in her seat so Jansen's hand fit better against her skin. He continued the gentle caressing farther up her leg until he reached the cuff of her shorts.

Jansen paused in his movement upwards and looked closer at Heidi. He did not want to take advantage of her in her semi-comatose state but he knew that she needed some release to see that she could still feel passion.

Heidi had leaned back in her seat and had closed her eyes. Her lips parted slightly as her breath came in ragged puffs. Jansen slid his hand under the soft material of Heidi's shorts. He could feel the dampness soaking through her panties. She was so hot and needy. Jansen caressed the cotton material lightly. Another groan, this one stronger and more urgent, rumbled deep in Heidi's throat. Jansen pushed aside the soft cloth to tangle his fingers in Heidi's hair. His knuckles brushed softly against her nub. Heidi strained against his hand in response.

Slowly, seductively, Jansen rubbed the wet nub. Heidi thrust her hips upwards to give Jansen better access. He slipped one finger between her folds, entering her a little before pulling away.

Heidi grabbed Jansen's hand and pushed him closer to her throbbing heat. Jansen responded, slipping his finger deeper between her folds. He lazily stroked Heidi, drawing his finger in and out with painstakingly slowness. Heidi's breathing became even more ragged as the ecstasy that Jansen's finger was invoking crashed through her body. She moved against his hand, trying to open herself even more to him.

Jansen could feel Heidi growing tight around his finger. He stroked faster, quietly encouraging Heidi's orgasm. Frenzied groans filled the car as Heidi came closer and closer to release. She held onto his arm with a white-knuckled grip as her body convulsed in pleasure. Her release came with one final, deep thrust and a fiery scream.

Chapter Fourteen

A knock on the door broke into Heidi's stupor. She shook her head in an attempt to clear away the lingering cobwebs. With coffee mug in hand, Heidi padded towards the front door. She took in a deep breath of air before reaching out with a shaking hand to turn the doorknob. She almost dreaded opening the door and seeing who was standing on her front porch. Silently she prayed that it would not be Jansen. Heidi did not think that she could face him yet. Not this early in the morning. And not after last night.

"Good morning sweetie," greeted Gladys cheerfully as the door swung open. She was wearing a pale blue, fitted sweat suit and had pulled her hair back from her face with a matching headband. Weights were strapped to each wrist and ankle. Gladys' beaming face was immediately filled with concern when she saw the bedraggled appearance of her daughter. "Darling! What's the matter? What's happened? You look dreadful."

"Morning, Gladys," Heidi said as she stepped back to let her mother in. "Nothing's the matter. I just didn't sleep much at all last night."

"Is something the matter?" asked Gladys, studying Heidi closely. There were large, purple smudges under Heidi's eyes and her hair looked like a family of mice had set up residence. Her lavender terry cloth robe hung loosely from her shoulders, not quite covering the wrinkled T-shirt and cotton shorts that Heidi wore underneath.

"No, not really," said Heidi. She led the way back to the kitchen where she poured a cup of coffee for her mother and topped up her own mug. "I guess I'm just more worked up over all this unpacking and trying to find a place for everything than I thought."

"Are you sure that's all that's bothering you?" Gladys took a sip of her coffee as she continued to study Heidi. Worry creased her face. "You have been spending an awful lot of time with Jansen this past week. Are you sure that that doesn't have something to do with it?"

"Why would it? We're just friends." Heidi jumped up from the table and walked over to the sink. She could not stand sitting across from Gladys and being scrutinized so closely. Instead, she turned on the taps with the pretence of planning to wash the stack of dirty dishes beside the sink.

"I think that it's a little more than friendship dear," said Gladys. "I can see the way you two look at each other. And you could light the Fourth of July fireworks with the heat between the two of you."

Heidi snorted softly, shaking her head in denial. "I think you have the wrong two people, Gladys. There isn't anything going on between me and Jansen."

Gladys lifted her mug to her lips and took a sip of the steaming coffee. She watched Heidi for a moment trying to concentrate on washing dishes but failing miserably. She knew that something very important was troubling her daughter. Something she understood all too well herself. "You may not think so but Jansen has other ideas. And hopes. He wants you. I can see it in his eyes whenever he looks at you. I have never seen eyes filled with such obvious desire as that pair. I wish someone would look at me like that. I wouldn't think twice about jumping into bed with him."

"Mother!" Heidi cried. She could not believe what she was hearing.

"What?" asked Gladys innocently. "I'm a woman and I have needs just like you. It's been awhile since I have been thoroughly loved by a man."

"I can't believe that I am having this conversation with my mother," muttered Heidi. She turned back to the sink overflowing with suds and grabbed her coffee cup to wash. "Of all the things to talk about with my mother, sex is definitely no where near being on my list."

Gladys watched Heidi as she tackled the pile of dirty dishes beside her. She noticed the droop to Heidi's shoulders. Usually, her daughter carried herself so proudly. Gladys toyed with her coffee mug, searching for a way to broach the painful subject that she believed was at the root of Heidi's distress. Finally, she decided the only way was to plunge right in.

"I never thought I would survive when your father died," Gladys began, pain filling her voice and giving it a husky quality. She took a deep breath before continuing. "Even though we didn't have the best of relationships at times, I didn't know how to live without him. I could feel myself shrivelling up inside. And the house made it seem so much worse. It was so empty and silent. A whisper would echo. You were away in school so there was no one left. I felt like everyone I loved had abandoned me. I forgot how to function."

Gladys stopped to take a sip of coffee to try to wet her suddenly dry throat. Heidi dropped her dishcloth into the water and joined her mother at the table. They had never talked much about her father after he had died. It had been a painful subject for both of them. Now, Heidi wondered why her mother was opening up. Was something the matter with her? Was she going to lose her mother too?

With a small sniffle, Gladys continued, "I almost gave up living completely. If it wasn't for John's father, your grandfather, I don't think I would have made it to the end of the year. He told me to stop grieving for what I had lost and start being thankful for what I had. Of course," Gladys chuckled softly, "he didn't put it quite so nicely. And then he showed me pictures of you. He said that I still had you to live for. To be strong for. You hadn't left me yet. But if I wasn't careful, I would lose you to, he said."

Gladys reached over and grasped Heidi's hand. She gave it a gentle squeeze as tears rolled down their cheeks. "The one thing that I remember most is that he said we are put on this earth for such a short time. If we are lucky, we will love once. If we are really lucky and truly blessed, we will love over and over. He said that John would always be a part of me. He would be my own personal guardian angel to help me live again. To guide me along the road until it was our time to meet again."

Gladys cupped Heidi's face in her hand. With her thumb, she brushed the tears from Heidi's cheek. In a voice filled with emotion, Gladys said, "Heidi, baby. Dean would not want to see you like this. He would want you to be happy. To be loved. To love. He would want you to live for him. Not die because of him."

Chapter Fifteen

Heidi pulled absent-mindedly at the weeds sticking up among the flowers surrounding her cottage. Her hands worked more from instinct than from direction. A thousand thoughts raced through her mind, and they all seemed to be centred around Jansen. She just could not get him out of her head, no matter how hard she tried. Everything around her, everything she did was starting to remind her of him.

She could still feel his hands on her, brushing lightly across her skin. His arms felt so strong. And safe. He had sent shivers coursing through her body with his gentle kisses. It was more than a physical response to the man's handsome looks. It went deeper and touched emotions in Heidi that had long been buried. These feelings scared her. Heidi had not felt this way since Dean. And she had thought that she would never feel this way again with anyone.

That was why she pushed him away. The feel of his body pressed against hers brought all the terrible memories flooding back. The police coming to her door. The morgue.

The funeral. They were memories that she had not wanted to relive, especially standing in the arms of Jansen.

"Oh, Dean," Heidi sighed, pulling up a weed from among the pansies. "Why did you have to leave me? Why did you have to go? How am I ever going to survive?"

"Does pulling them out by their roots help to wring an answer from them?" asked a deep voice from behind Heidi. Heidi jumped at the sound of the voice. She had not heard anyone come into the small garden alongside the cottage. She half turned to watch Jansen come closer, a confused look replacing the sadness for a brief moment. "The pansies I mean. You seemed to have pulled a few out with the weeds."

"Oh!" Heidi looked down at the crushed purple flower in her hand. "I'm not paying very good attention to what I am doing. I'm a little distracted I guess."

"Was it a good distraction? Maybe about the other night?" Jansen asked, a little teasing note to his voice. He knelt down beside Heidi and pulled at a few weeds pushing up between the flowers.

Colour crept up Heidi's cheeks. She turned her head quickly to hide her reaction. But it was not quite quick enough. Jansen chuckled at Heidi's red face.

"I was just thinking about...about..." Heidi's voice trailed off. She just could not bring herself to tell Jansen about Dean.

"Were you thinking about Dean?" Jansen asked quietly.

Heidi whirled around, a shocked expression covering her face. She stammered, "How...how do you know about Dean?"

"You were talking to Dean when I came up the walk. I assumed you were talking out loud to him. Either that, or you named all your pansies Dean." Jansen nodded at the pansies in the bed at Heidi's feet. She followed his gaze, colouring again when she saw the ruined flowers.

"Oh! Stupid me. Of course you would have heard me say his name."

"Also, your mom told me little about him," Jansen admitted sheepishly. He settled on a stone bench to watch Heidi put away her gardening tools a little too aggressively. Instead of fitting neatly into the basket, shovels, trowels, and even a few unlucky pansies stuck out over the sides every which way.

"She what!?" Heidi exclaimed. A tough of panic filled her voice. "Oh, that meddlesome old woman. Why can't she just mind her own business?" Heidi seethed at the thought of her mother spilling her life story. She did not want every stranger knowing how sad her life was. She wanted to be able to grieve alone, without anyone feeling sorry for her.

Jansen did not want Heidi to blame her mother for something that she was not completely responsible for. Even though he knew more details about Dean and his death than either Heidi or Gladys did, Jansen had wanted to get a perspective on how the tragedy had impacted

Heidi and her emotional state. He quickly confessed his involvement as mush as he could before too many feathers were ruffled. "Actually, she didn't want to tell my anything at first. She said something about it not being her place. But my charm won her over. I had to know how you felt. After the other night, I was afraid that it was something I had done to make you push me away."

Heidi looked over at where Jansen sat stretched out on the stone bench beside the open doorway. The way he sat, with his long legs stretched out in front of him as he leaned back against the brick wall, reminded her of a cat basking in the sun. The image of those long legs wrapped around her flitted through her mind. She shook her head to clear it. Now was not the time. She sighed deeply and sat down on the bench beside Jansen. "What did my mom tell you?"

Jansen looked over at Heidi before answering. She looked so worn and beat up, as if she had been battling some unknown demon. "Just that you and Dean had been inseparable since high school. And that after moving apart during university, you met up one day and decided that you still couldn't live without each other."

"Did she tell you about how Dean…died?" Heidi stumbled over the word. It was still hard for her to say the word out loud, even after almost two years.

"A little. She said that he had been jogging in the park and was mugged," Jansen said simply. Gladys had told him the entire story but he wanted to hear it from Heidi. He wanted her to say tell it so that maybe she could start healing. She had kept everything bottled up for so long. It was time for her to let it go.

"I can still remember exactly how I felt when the police came to tell me that Dean wasn't coming back anymore. A piece of me died that day with him. The hardest thing that I ever had to do was to go to the morgue and identify his b-body," Heidi stammered. She closed her eyes for a minute and took a deep breath before continuing. Now that she had started, she could not stop herself from going over every detail. As she continued, it felt as if the tight band squeezing her soul slowly eased the pressure. "All the way there, I wished that it wouldn't be him. I made promises with God that if he just made it all some terrible nightmare, I would do anything. Anything. Seeing Dean there covered by a sheet really hit me hard. I couldn't pretend any longer. It was brutal what they did to him. I almost couldn't recognise him the way they had bashed his head. And...and seeing how they had scalped him. He had such thick, wavy brown hair. I used to love running my fingers though his hair."

Heidi broke down, the sobs wracking though her body, with the pain of the memories. Jansen wrapped a protective arm around her and laid her head on his shoulder. He gently stroked her hair as he waited until the sobs slowed in intensity. They sat like this until the sun had moved high overhead.

"You okay?" Jansen asked, looking down at Heidi.

"I...I think so. I'm sorry I broke down like that." Heidi

pulled a tissue from her pocket and blew her nose. She tried to push herself away, to regain her composure, but Jansen gently tugged her back. He laid his cheek on the top of her head and held her close.

"It's okay. It's obvious that you needed that. You've been keeping it all bottled up for too long," Jansen murmured against her hair. His breath tickled her ear, sending shivers down her back.

Heidi sighed softly and snuggled into Jansen's arms. It had been too long since she had just been held. "I've had to be strong for my mom and for Dean's family. I had to arrange everything and make sure that everything was settled."

"Well, it's time you thought about yourself. You don't have to be strong for me. No one is here to see you, so let it out," Jansen said. He pulled Heidi tighter against himself for a moment, trying to reassure her with his actions that everything would be okay. More than anything, he wished he could erase all the pain and anguish that Heidi had felt for the past two years. He wished that he could do more than just hold her close.

"It has helped to cry," Heidi admitted. "I've been trying to push it all away for so long now."

"Do the police know who killed Dean?" Jansen asked, casually.

Heidi shook her head. There was frustration in her voice when she answered. "They don't have very many leads. It was too early in the morning for there to be very many witnesses out yet. They think that it was some gang initiation by the way they cut him up. And they figure that there had to be three or four guys. There weren't many signs of struggle on Dean so they figure that a couple of guys had to have held him down."

"Well, I am sure that the police will find the guys soon." Jansen tried to sound encouraging. He just hoped that he was right and Heidi's nightmare would end soon. "If it was some sort of gang initiation, then they are bound to repeat it. Maybe next time someone will see them."

"I hope so. I want those thugs to pay for what they did to Dean." Heidi tensed in Jansen's arms as the anger mixed with the pain.

Jansen tipped up Heidi's chin so that he could look into her eyes. He searched their depths, looking for the sunshine hidden among the shadows. "Are you okay now? Do you feel like dinner? I know a great little spot just down the highway a little ways that serves the best food you will ever find. My treat."

"Oh, I don't know. I'm sure that I look like a wreck after crying all over you."

"You look beautiful," Jansen reassured her. "Don't ever be afraid to cry."

Heidi sat back to take a good look at Jansen. She simply smiled and shook her head.

"What was that look for?" Jansen asked.

"You never fail to amaze me," Heidi said simply.

"Ah, I am finally rubbing off on you!" Jansen crowed. A

wide smile split his face. "My charm is working. I told you, there is no woman who can resist it! So, how about dinner?"

"Okay," Heidi sighed. She reached up to run a hand through her hair. "Eating any place but at the inn sounds good right now. I don't think I could face my mother right now without causing some sort of scene. Just give me half an hour to freshen up."

"Sounds good. I'll stop by in half an hour to pick you up. Wear something comfortable and roomy. Where we're going, you'll need it!" Jansen instructed with a twinkle in his eye. He winked at Heidi before turning to go.

Heidi watched as Jansen strolled back down the path, whistling off key. She sat there until he disappeared among the pine trees and then rose to wash her face and change.

Chapter Sixteen

"Are you sure you know where you are?" Heidi asked as the miles slipped behind them and they moved farther away from Hadey's Cove. "We've been driving for awhile. I thought you said the place is just down the highway a little ways."

"It is. And we're almost there," answered Jansen. He glanced over at Heidi sitting in the seat beside him. There was a mysterious grin on his face and his eyes twinkled with excitement. He was acting like a little boy on Christmas morning eager to start ripping open presents.

"There doesn't seem to be much civilisation around here. Are you sure you know where you're going?" Heidi asked for the second time. She looked out her window at the dense forest flashing by. All she had seen for the last ten minutes were trees. Not one single building. Not even a road that could lead to a building. And if remembered correctly from her childhood, it was a long time before this road led to any sign of life.

"Yup. A man always knows where he is going." Jansen puffed out his chest in mock male pride. The silly grin on his face, however, ruined the attempt at male bravado. "The place is off the road a bit so it can be hard to see."

"How did you find this place then?" Heidi asked. She was growing more concerned as the miles slipped by. Just where was Jansen taking her?

Jansen chuckled softly. He was enjoying this way too much. The glare Heidi gave him caused his chuckle to deepen and grow louder. It threatened to turn into all out laughter. "With a little bit of luck and a whole lot of clumsiness! I sort of stumbled upon it one day when I was out for a hike. I think you'll like it. It's quaint and peaceful. A great place to get away from everything. It's actually not far from Hadey's Cove when you're hiking. But you have to take a more round about way to get there when driving."

Heidi was still unconvinced. Only when she saw the building in front of her would she believe that Jansen knew where he was going. "Sounds perfect. What kind of food do they serve?"

"Anything and everything. You can have almost anything you want."

"Even lobster bisque in a cream reduction sauce?" Heidi asked, one eyebrow arched upwards in question.

Jansen chuckled, nodding his head in agreement. "Yup. Even lobster bisque in whatever you just said."

"This place sounds almost too good to be true. I can hardly wait to get there." There was still a note of scepticism in her voice. She looked out the window again, scanning the dense forest for any sign of habitation.

Jansen glanced over at Heidi briefly. He smiled to himself at the sight of her furrowed brow. This little trip was working to take her mind off Dean and the pain she still felt so deeply over his death. Spotting their turn-off, Jansen slowed the truck and flipped on his turn signal. "We are almost there now. It's just a little ways down this road."

Jansen turned off onto a dirt road barely visible among the towering trees. It was not much more than two ruts cut out from among the ferns and undergrowth. Spring runoff had cut deep groves along the road, making the going rough. Jansen slowed the truck right down to a crawl as they jostled over the first few bumps. He had borrowed the truck from Gladys since he knew that Gord's car would never have been able to handle the little bit of off-roading that they had to do. Gladys had been more than happy to trade vehicles for the night and had been eager to tour the town in the splashy yellow sports car.

"This place is definitely out of the way. How could anyone ever find it?" Heidi grimaced as the truck hit a large hole and she bumped her head on the roof.

Jansen stole a quick glance at Heidi to see how she was fairing before returning his eyes to the road. He did not dare to look away from the road in front of him for too long in case he missed a rut or hole.

"It's part of the charm of this place. It's unspoiled by the masses." Jansen gestured at the tall, thick trees pressing up on either side of them. "When you find the place once, you never forget it and never want to share it with anyone else. It keeps drawing you back to it."

"If you never want to share it, why are you sharing it with me?" Heidi winced as another hole sent her heavily into the door. She rubbed her knee where it had bumped into the window crank.

"Well, it's the kind of place where you want to take someone special. Someone who is as beautiful as the place itself," Jansen explained. His cheeks coloured slightly at the sound of passion in his voice. "We are almost there now so close your eyes. I want it to be a surprise. No peeking now!"

Heidi closed her eyes and covered her them with her hand to show that there would be no chance of her sneaking a peak. She felt like a little girl again, waiting for a big surprise. She wondered what could be so special about this place for it to be so out of the way and such a big secret. How could the business survive if the average person driving down the highway could not find it? She felt the truck come to a stop. Heidi asked, "Can I look now?"

"Not yet. Just sit tight for a minute and I'll come around to help you out."

Jansen shut the truck off and then hopped out. He paused for a moment to look around him. A wave of peacefulness washed over him. He had never seen anything so beautiful. Except for Heidi. She had taken his breath away as soon as he had laid eyes on her, just like this place. It had not just been her physical beauty that had struck him, but also her soul that had shown through. Even though he could see that something troubled her, he knew that beneath all the pain, there was love and happiness waiting to break through, waiting for a second chance. He had wanted to grab her up and chase away that pain from the first moment.

Maybe this will help her to start seeing the beauty in life again, thought Jansen. He walked around the truck to where Heidi sat waiting for him.

"Okay, girl. Be prepared to be amazed! Just let me help you out of the truck. No looking yet though," Jansen warned. He checked that Heidi still had her eyes closed tight.

Heidi climbed out gingerly, unsure of what she was stepping onto. Jansen's arm went around her waist to guide her to the ground.

"Now, take my arm and I'll move you over a bit so that you can see everything when you open your eyes." Jansen reached for her hand and gently laid it across his bent arm.

"I feel so silly. No one's watching me are they?" Heidi asked as she linked arms with Jansen. They moved together a short ways away from the truck.

"Don't worry. It's just you and me," he whispered.

Jansen stopped and let go of Heidi's hand. He moved slightly away from her to give her some room. "Okay. You can open you eyes now."

Heidi's eyes fluttered open. For a minute, she was blinded by the bright sun after being in darkness for so long, but as soon as her eyes grew accustomed to the light, she was amazed by what she saw.

Sun played off a clear, ice blue pool of water. A large tree extended its branches over the pool, as if reaching out for the coolness of the water. Long ago, someone had tied a knotted rope to one of the limps for swinging into the pool's icy depths. It was tied loosely to a peg driven into the tree's trunk, waiting for someone to come along and swing on it once more. A small slice of sand invited guests to bury their toes in its whiteness along the pool's edge. There was just enough room for two people to stretch out in the afternoon sun. Nothing marred the surface of the water except for at one end where the water trickled over shiny black rocks to the lake below.

"It's beautiful," whispered Heidi, afraid to break the peace. "How did you find this place? I never knew it existed."

"I got to talking to a few old locals at the coffee shop one day. They told me of a place where they used to go as young boys, and later, as teenagers with their girlfriends. This used to be the make-out spot before there were such things as drive-ins," explained Jansen. He smiled as he remembered some of the stories that he had been told. "It's amazing some of the things those guys used to do!"

Heidi walked to the little beach and kicked her shoes off. She buried her toes in the sand, enjoying the coolness against her skin. As she looked around her, a far away look filled her eyes. She became oblivious to the environment around her, losing herself in her memories.

Jansen picked up the wicker picnic basket he had hidden among the ferns earlier and sat down on a fallen tree at the edge of the grass. He watched Heidi intently. He knew that she was somewhere else right now. He just wished that he knew where and that he could be there with her. He wanted to pick her up and shield her from the pain and hurt that haunted her.

A haunting, far away call from an unknown bird brought Heidi back to the present. She shook herself gently to clear the lingering memories. She glanced over her shoulder to where Jansen sat watching her.

"Whatcha got there?" Heidi asked, spotting the basket at Jansen's feet. Her stomach growled in curious anticipation.

"Oh, just a little something to nibble on," Jansen said. He reached into the basket and pulled out a brightly stripped blanket. "I thought that we could have a little picnic before we went back. I can't take anymore of Gladys' healthy food. I need some grease and sugar and fat before I turn into one big nut! I thought that this would be a perfect excuse to indulge the devil in me."

"So what do you have in there? Not a lump of lard I hope!" The thought of grease and sugar drew Heidi closer. She, too, had missed junk food in the last few days. She had planned to stock her cottage with all her favourite snack foods but packing, and Jansen, had been taking up so much of her time lately that she had not been able to make it to the grocery store yet.

"Nope." Jansen shook his head as he continued to pull out containers. As he set each one down, he explained what was inside, "but the next best thing! Fried chicken, deep fried jalapeno cheese poppers, celery sticks, chilli fries, and triple chocolate cake."

"Ummm... Sounds tempting." Heidi arched an eyebrow at the tub full of celery sticks filled with cheese and raisins and asked, "but wouldn't celery sticks be classified as healthy food?"

"It is." Jansen shrugged, an apologetic look on his face. "I had to throw something in to help soak up all the grease. And the guilt. Now sit down here and help me polish off this food. If I'm going to have a grease-induced heart attack, I'm not going to be the only one. I'm going to bring someone down with me."

Heidi laughed at the idea and settled down on the blanket beside Jansen. She reached across the blanket and pulled a thermal container closer to herself. The smell of fried chicken greeted her nose as she pulled off the lid. She sighed happily.

"Mmmm... It does smell good." Heidi took a deep breath, enjoying the tantalizing aroma wafting from the container. "Let me guess. Uncle Bert's special fried chicken?"

"How did you know?" asked Jansen, surprised.

"I grew up on this chicken. I would know the smell anywhere."

Heidi and Jansen fell into a comfortable silence as they dug into the food. Occasionally, someone would make a comment, sending them both into fits of laughter. Their giddiness was aided by a bottle of ice wine that Jansen pulled out of the water like a magician pulling a rabbit from his hat.

Once all the food was eaten and the empty dishes packed neatly back into the picnic basket, Heidi stretched out on the blanket, sighing contentedly. She watched the clouds gently rolling across the sky.

"See anything interesting up there," asked Jansen.

"Just trying to pick out shapes in the clouds. See that fish over there above the tree?" Heidi pointed up to the spot that she was referring to.

Jansen laid down beside Heidi and put his head close to hers. His gaze followed Heidi's hand as he searched for the fish in the sky. Heidi turned her head slightly so that she could see Jansen better. He had his face turned towards the sky, searching for other funny shaped clouds, so she had a good view of his profile. His features looked as if they had been carefully crafted from the finest granite. His jaw was strong and just slightly square. The first hints of a five o'clock shadow were just beginning to spread over it. His lips, plump and kissable, were curved up in a contented smile. A tiny bump marred his otherwise straight nose, hinting at a past break that had not been quite properly set. Heidi could see the beginnings of crow's feet at the corner of Jansen's eye. They only added to the character of his face instead of showing age. A tiny scar just above his eyebrow caught her attention. She had never noticed it before and only saw it now because she was just inches away. She caught herself just in time before she could reach up and run a finger along the pale white line.

"Oh yeah. There it is. Cool. And there's a big fishing boat coming to catch it." Jansen pointed to a cloud drifting cross the sky behind the fish. "Swim little fishy, swim. The big, bad boat is going to get you and gobble you up for dinner."

"Where?" Heidi asked, laughing at Jansen's sudden enthusiasm. She turned her head to look back up at the sky. "I don't see any boat."

"Just on the other side of the tree. The big triangle with the stick coming out of it." Jansen leaned over closer to Heidi to point out the cloud for her. He caught the scent of the fruity shampoo that she used to wash her hair with. Strawberry banana. The smell sent his libido into overdrive.

Heidi snorted in mock contempt. She frowned at Jansen as if he had suddenly misbehaved. "That looks more like an upside down umbrella."

"If you want it to be." Jansen shrugged his shoulders, or shrugged as much as he could while still lying flat on his back. He stuck his nose further up in the air over protest of Heidi's reaction. "I think that it looks like a boat with its sail down."

Heidi playfully punched Jansen in the arm for his pout. He returned her jab with a poke in the ribs.

"There's a big apple." Heidi pointed at the cloud directly above them.

"That cloud looks like a pizza with a slice missing from it."

"You're crazy. It's a pretty funny shaped pizza."

"Maybe. But it kinda looks like pizza when I make it." Jansen shifted slightly on the blanket as the rock digging into his shoulder started to get uncomfortable. He sighed softly. "I haven't done this for awhile so I'm a little rusty."

"Hmmm...me neither," Heidi agreed. "I haven't seen so much blue sky for awhile either."

Jansen looked over at Heidi from the corner of his eye to see how she was doing. "It's been fun though. I like this. Just lying here enjoying the day. I don't do it near enough."

"Does anyone really anymore?" Heidi asked softly. Pain flickered through her eyes but was quickly masked by something that Jansen could not quite read.

"No. Not really. Once we grow up, we think we don't have time to just sit and do nothing."

"It's sad really. Life's too short not to enjoy it."

Jansen rolled to his side and propped his head up so that he could look at Heidi better. He could see pain in her cat green eyes. He gently pulled her head toward him so that she was forced to look at him. "My sweet Heidi," he whispered as he dipped his head down and gently brushed Heidi's lips with his own. Her lips were tentative, almost shy. Jansen coaxed a response from her until he could feel Heidi returning the kiss. Slowly, he reached over and lightly ran his hand down her side until it rested on her hip. He bent a little closer to deepen the kiss. As his tongue tickled her lips apart, he moved his hand across her belly. It continued its exploration until it gently cupped her left breast. Jansen rubbed Heidi's nipple with his thumb until he could feel the hard bud beneath her shirt. He pulled slightly away from Heidi and took the nipple in his mouth. He suckled it, tugging at it with his teeth.

Heidi squirmed at the sensations Jansen was sending through her body and moaned softly. The sound startled Heidi and brought her crashing back to reality. She grew rigid under Jansen's hands.

Jansen felt the change in Heidi immediately. He lifted his head and looked into her eyes. The pain had been replaced by panic. He swore to himself and rolled away. He ran his hands roughly through his hair as he tried to compose himself.

"I'm sorry, Heidi," Jansen said. "I shouldn't have done that. I got caught up in the moment and forgot where I was for a minute."

"It's okay. I didn't mean to react like that. I've just gone through a rough time and am a little gun shy right now." Heidi sat up on the blanket and hugged her knees to her chest. She was starting to feel childish around Jansen, eagerly accepting his kisses and his touches one minute and then pushing him away when she could not take the intensity of the emotions that he stirred in her anymore.

Jansen felt a little frustrated. Frustrated at himself and frustrated at the world. He could not seem to stop himself from pawing at Heidi like a hormone-ridden teenager. And life was too unfair for dealing Heidi such a cruel hand. Jansen ran a hand through his hair as he tried to come up with the words to explain his actions to Heidi. "I know that something is bothering you so that makes what I did even worse. I just can't help it though. I am really attracted to you, Heidi. You fill my every waking moment and are always in my dreams. I can't get you out of my head. I've tried to stay away. To give you some space. But I keep being drawn back to you. It's like a moth being drawn to a flame. I know it's dangerous but I just can't stay away."

"I like you too, Jansen. And I do value your friendship. Getting to know you these past few weeks has helped to make life a little brighter. I don't want to lose that." Heidi reached over and gave Jansen's hand a reassuring squeeze. Jansen had bought a little bit of sunshine into Heidi's life lately. She did not want to lose that because of her insecurities. "You've given me hope that I can deal with the turns my life may take."

"I don't want to lose your friendship either. I just can't help myself sometimes. It's a male thing you now." A smile tugged at the corners of Jansen's mouth. Heidi answered with a chuckle, helping to relieve some tension. "Let's go for a swim. That rope swing looks like it could be fun."

Heidi looked down at the tan cotton shorts and turquoise tank top she was wearing. She shook her head slowly. "I don't have a bathing suit on or one with me. I wasn't told that be would be going in the water."

"Got that covered. I took the liberty of picking something up for you in town," said Jansen. He quickly added when he saw the look of horror flood Heidi's face, "Don't worry. It's decent. A one piece tank suit like all the Olympic swimmers are sporting these days. Covers a person from chin to ankle and leaves absolutely no room for the imagination."

"But how do you know my size?" Heidi asked, still not quite convinced.

"I am a great observer of details. I pay attention to the little things around me. It's part of my job and has pretty much become second nature for me." Jansen grinned sheepishly as he added almost as an afterthought, "And I asked your mom."

Jansen pulled a shopping bag from behind the tree where the picnic basket had been. He handed a celery green bathing suit to Heidi and kept a pair of grey swim trunks for himself. They found separate trees a discrete distance away from each other to change behind. Jansen was the first to finish changing and headed for the rope swing. He took a mighty running jump and hollered like a wild man as he swung out over the water. Just before he started to swing back, he let go of the rope and dropped into the water with a big splash. Meanwhile, Heidi had slipped into the water and was watching Jansen revert to his inner child. She laughed at the gleeful look on his face when he resurfaced.

Jansen and Heidi took turns jumping into the water from the old rope. They splashed and dunked each other until the sun dipped low in the sky. Exhausted, they flopped back on the sand and watched the sun set while they dried off. Jansen wrapped an arm around Heidi and she leaned her head against his shoulder. They sat quietly; simply enjoying each other until the first stars appeared in the evening sky.

Chapter Seventeen

The evening crowd was starting to fill up the bar, making it a loud and bustling place. It was ten-cent wings night, meaning everyone in town was congregating to enjoy cheap wings and good company.

Jansen had settled in booth at the back of the room the opposite corner from the blaring jukebox. A half-empty mug of beer sat on the table in front of him. He idly wiped the condensation from the mug as he watched the people milling around him. A few of the townspeople nodded a greeting as they passed by the table. The growing crowd and the noise it was generating was the perfect place to hold a meeting. No one would be able to easily hear their conversation and if they did hear snippets, they would not be able to understand the gist of the discussion. Now, if only his partner would show up, Jansen would be able to have the meeting.

Just as Jansen was starting to give up hope that Gord was going to show up, he breezed in. Weaving his way through the crowd, Gord reached the table slightly breathless. He plopped down on the cushioned seat across from Jansen and reaching for the mug on the table, downed the remaining beer in one gulp.

"Please, help yourself," Jansen said, sarcastically, as he watched his partner finish of his drink. "I wasn't going to finish that myself or anything."

"Ahh...that's just what I needed," said Gord, wearing a trace of froth from his upper lip. He waved at a passing waitress to bring another round for the table. After the waitress set to new mugs of frothy beers and a bowl of salted peanuts on the table, Gord handed over a plain manila folder to Jansen. "I think you'll be eager to see what's in here."

Jansen took the folder from Gord and opened it up on the front table. He scanned the pages quickly, saying very little as he read what they said. When he finished reading the file, he closed the cover and pushed the folder back towards his partner. He took a sip of his beer as he let the information sink in. "Thanks for updating me on the case, Gord. It's good to know that we're finally goina be making a move. Maybe we'll finally be able to put an end to all this horror."

"Yeah, two years of hard work is finally paying off. Of course, this means you're going to be needed back in the city." Gord watched his partner, gauging his reaction.

"It'll be good to get back and get into the swing of things again," Jansen said, his voice void of any enthusiasm. "I've been on vacation for too long now."

"Ah, a vacation can never be too long. Especially in a great little place like this with all its intriguing sights." As much as he hinted, his buddy just was not taking the bait. Gord decided to try another, slightly more direct, approach to finding out what he was interested in. "I was a little surprised when you suggested meeting here. I thought you and Heidi would have plans or something on a Friday night so you would only have time for a quick chat at the inn while you got ready."

Jansen popped a couple of peanuts into his mouth. There were so many reasons for needing to get away from the inn, and Heidi was at the root of all of them. Mostly he needed to get away for a little while to clear his head and to try to get his thoughts in order. He had spent an incredible day with Heidi. Life almost felt normal for a time. But now, in the light of a new day, Jansen was confused. He did not understand what he was feeling or the draw that kept pulling him towards Heidi.

Not sure how to explain everything to Gord, Jansen choose to stick to the safe and easy explanation, "I thought we would have a little more privacy here. We wouldn't have to worry about Gladys or Heidi overhearing anything we were talking about."

"Ohhh...so you want to talk about Heidi?" Gord asked gleefully. He rubbed his hands together and leaned over the table, closer to Jansen. He was excited as a schoolgirl with a juicy secret about the football star to tell. Finally they were getting to what he really wanted to know more about. "Does she look as hot without her clothes on as she does with?"

Jansen was immediately put on edge. Gord's raunchiness hit a nerve. Heidi was more than a one night stand. She was a very special person who deserved only the best things that the world has to offer. And Jansen was not sure that he was the one to offer the world to Heidi. He had too much history, too much baggage. And his job was not conducive to a relationship.

"First of all, I meant I didn't want Heidi or Gladys hearing us talk about the case. And second of all, there is nothing between me and Heidi."

"Oh, come on man." Gord threw a crumbled up napkin at Jansen. "I've seen the way you two look at each other. There's more sparks there than a Fourth of July fireworks display."

"I admit that I care for Heidi. More than I probably should. But there's no room in my life for a woman or a relationship," Jansen said. He tossed the napkin back on the table in frustration.

"Why not? If you care for her, and I think it's more than just 'care', why wouldn't you want her in your life?" Gord studied his partner for a minute. He understood all the insecurities that Jansen was feeling. He felt it every time he went out with someone. Because of them, Gord would never let himself get too close to a woman. He skipped out on any relationship before it got too serious. "You are a great judge of character so she must be pretty special to have you all tied up in knots. What's stopping you from going after her?"

"Well, my involvement in this case for starters." Jansen hesitated slightly. A thousand reasons came to mind but they all centred around one thing. "But mostly my job."

"What's wrong with your job? It's an honest living."

Jansen took a minute to answer Gord. He tried to organise his thoughts a little so he could explain clearly what he was feeling. "But it can also be very dangerous. I can't put anyone in harms way just because they are connected to me. Look at Parker. He got involved with some nasty business and lost his wife and kids because of it. I couldn't make someone I love a possible target."

"So you do love her."

"I don't know." Jansen shook his head slowly. He reached for his beer mug and gulped the remaining fluid in one big mouthful. His mouth was suddenly very dry, as if it was full of cotton. "I do know that I can't stop thinking about her. She's there when I go to sleep at night and she's there when I walk up in the morning. I just can't seem to get enough of her. I use every excuse possible to see her. And some of them are pretty lame."

Gord chuckled. He was happy to see his friend in this predicament. It was time for him to find some happiness with a special person. Jansen had put so many people before himself for a long time now. It was his turn to put himself first. "Yup, sounds like love to me. You, my friend, are one hundred percent certifiably in love. You are a goner."

"I don't want anything bad to ever happen to Heidi again. Which is why I can't have a relationship with her. Never mind what she will think when she learns my involvement in her late husband's case."

Gord signalled for another round of drinks. He waited for the waitress to return with a couple of fresh mugs of beer before continuing the conversation. "I think you are underestimating that incredible lady. She loves you right back, even though she may be farther from knowing it than you were." Gord lazily traced the ring of water left behind on the table by his beer mug. "You know, there is one solution to your employment problem."

"And what," Jansen asked, "is that?"

"Quit," Gord said simply.

"Quit?" Jansen snorted, almost choking on the mouthful of beer he had just taken.

"Yeah. Quit." Gord repeated himself. As far as he was concerned, it was a simple solution to the problem. One that would benefit everyone. "Ever since I've known you, you have been dreaming about living in a small town and raising a big family. If my eyes are right, this is a small town. A nice, friendly one too. No weird axe murderers running around the streets as far as I can tell. It would be a perfect place to raise half a dozen or so little Jansens."

"I don't know." Jansen hesitated. His work had always been his life. Everything he did was related to his job. His job was who he was. Could he give it up without giving himself up? "This is a great place but..."

"No more buts," interrupted Gord. "You deserve to be happy. You have worked hard to make a good life for yourself. Now you should be sharing it with someone special. And Heidi makes you happy. I've never seen you so relaxed. Usually you're wound up tighter than a top. Heidi's good for you. If I was you, I would grab onto her and never let go."

Jansen still was not sure. There were so many unknowns. "It's not that easy though. We both have our own history. And Heidi has been through so much. Who even knows if she will ever be ready for another relationship."

"That girl is no nun, man." Gord pushed his empty mug away. He shook his head when a passing waitress asked if he was interested in another refill. "She may not be ready right now, but the right man and the right suggestions will change that. And you, sir, are that man."

"I don't know," Jansen said again. He was so unsure about everything when it came to Heidi. He was afraid of hurting her even more than she already was.

Gord gave Jansen one more push towards a new future. "Promise me one thing. You'll at least think about it. About pursuing a future with Heidi. You both deserve to be happy."

Chapter Eighteen

Heidi nestled further back among the pillows on the window seat as the storm continued to rage outside. Lightning flashes lit the sky, giving brief glimpses of the menacing clouds rolling overhead. Rain pelted down in torrents. The storm echoed the storm in Heidi's head and heart. She laid her forehead against the cool glass of the window, trying to stop the thoughts from entering.

"Oh, Dean. What is wrong with me? Why am I feeling this way about Jansen? I don't want to. I want to be faithful to you baby. You were my world. How can I want another man?" Heidi sobbed quietly. She desperately wished that Dean was with her right now. Then all the pain and heartache would go away. And everything would be simple again.

Socks, a stray grey tabby cat who had adopted Heidi, jumped onto the bench. He rubbed up against Heidi's leg and purred loudly. Absentmindedly, she reached over to scratch him behind the ears. He arched his back and flexed his claws under her caress.

Heidi looked down at the cat. She had not wanted a pet

but Socks had had different ideas. He had showed up one day and would not leave, no matter how much Heidi had tried to chase him away. He would always be at the doorstep in the morning waiting to get in. Finally, she had given up and let him stay. Heidi had grown used to Socks being around and was happy to have company now.

"Socks, why can't my life be as easy and uncomplicated as yours? All you have to do is worry about when you will be fed next. And by the looks of you, you don't worry about that too often."

Socks looked sideways at Heidi, almost as if he understood the jab Heidi was taking at his weight. He stood, stretched, and jumped onto the bookshelf above the window seat. As he landed, he brushed against an antique silver picture frame, sending it crashing to the floor. The glass shattered as it landed with a loud crash.

Heidi jumped up from her seat, sending pillows flying. She swatted at the cat before bending down to pick up the remnants of the frame. "Socks! You clumsy cat! That was my favourite frame. Get out of here before I throw you out in the storm."

Heidi knelt beside the pile of broken glass and frame. She gingerly picked up what remained of the old frame. Dean's grandma had given it to them as a wedding gift just before she passed away. Heidi turned the frame over to see if the picture had been hurt. The smiling face of Dean looked back up at her, unmarred by the fall. He had had the picture taken when they first started going out again after college and was living two hours away. He had told her, as he gave her the picture, that it would help to keep him close no matter how far apart they were. A solitary tear slipped down Heidi's cheek and landed on the picture. She carefully wiped it away with her thumb.

Heidi sighed. Everything was so different now, so mixed up. Shaking herself slightly in an attempt to clear some of the sadness away, Heidi looked down at the broken glass. "Well, I guess I had better get this mess cleaned up before I hurt myself. Maybe I can find someone to fix the frame for me. At least Dean's picture is okay."

Heidi stood up and turned towards the kitchen to get a broom. Just as she moved, something fell from her lap and fluttered to the floor. Puzzled, she bent over to pick it up. It was a small envelope with her name scrawled across the front. She immediately recognised the handwriting—it was Dean's. Forgetting the shards of broken glass on the floor, Heidi returned to her window seat with the envelope. She stared down at the yellowed envelope cradled in her hands for a long time before she finally turned it over. A riot of emotions raged through her body—fear, excitement, nervousness, curiosity. She could not remember tucking anything in behind Dean's picture, but if it had not been her, who then? And why was she finding it now?

The seal had been broken long ago but Heidi could see where the pressure from the frame had resealed the envelope. She gingerly tugged at the flap, not wanting to rip what may be inside. She found a letter tucked neatly inside. Heidi pulled it out and unfolded the single, lined page. It was a letter that Dean had written to her shortly before they had left for college, each going their separate ways.

> *Dear Heidi,*
>
> *I don't want to leave you darling, but I have to. Something is calling me and I must go. There is something out there waiting for me. I don't know what it is but I have to go find out. And you have to let go too, baby. We have to let go of each other no matter how much it hurts. I will always be near you, if not in body, in spirit. I love you, Heidi. I will always love you. Don't ever forget that. Whenever you need me, I will be there. Just look up at the North Star and think of me. I will be up there, watching over you, guiding you along life's path.*
>
> *I have to go now. I can't be near you for a while. My arms already ache with the desire to hold you. But we won't be apart forever. Someday we will meet again. We will walk in a beautiful garden and talk of old times. Love and laughter will surround us again and there will be no more pain. Remember that. Take that with you through the journey of life. We will be together again someday. But for now, enjoy life to its fullest. Live every*

day like a gift and don't turn any opportunity away. There is nothing that you can do that will ever hurt me.

If something good comes along, grab on and don't let go. Nothing should stop you from being happy, not even me. Do not be afraid to welcome new love into your life. Promise me this.

I love you baby. I will never forget you.

Dean

Heidi stared out the window into space for a long time. She felt the power of the words. It was almost as if Dean was releasing her and letting her live again. She had been living in the past for so long now. She had almost forgotten about the future.

"Thank you, Dean. Thank you for writing this letter. It still hurts not to have you near but maybe now I can start to let you go. With your blessing, I can go back to living." Heidi whispered as she looked into the storm. Even though she could not see the North Star, she knew that Dean was out there watching over her. He had promised and he would never break a promise.

Socks picked his way through the broken glass and jumped up into Heidi's lap. Heidi smiled down at the cat and ruffled his fur. "And thank you, Socks, for breaking this frame. I might never have found this letter if you weren't so clumsy and if you hadn't insisted on living here."

Chapter Nineteen

Heidi shook the rain from her coat as she stepped into the large entrance way. There were a few people milling around as the storm continued to rage outside. Heidi looked around her, searching for a familiar face.

Molly, the new receptionist, bustled up to Heidi. She fairly shook with nervous energy. This was her first job and even after being at the inn for over a month, she was still afraid of doing something wrong. "Good evening, Miss Heidi. You shouldn't be out in this weather! It is storming something fierce out there."

"Evening, Molly. I'm looking for Jansen Winfield. Have you seen him around by chance?" Heidi asked the receptionist as she continued to look around her.

"He left this morning, ma'am." Molly shook her head in emphasis. "Just before the storm hit again. He said something about having to get back to work or something."

"Shoot! I really needed to talk to him." Heidi stamped her foot. She knew she should have come over last night but, because of the late hour, had been afraid of waking someone up. And it had taken the rest of the night to work up her nerve to tell Jansen what she was feeling and to ask him if he would to give them a chance.

"Maybe Miss Gladys will know how to get in touch with him. Mr. Jansen had breakfast with her right before he left. She's in the library now," Molly suggested quickly. Heidi's sudden outburst made her nervous.

"Thanks, Molly," Heidi called over her shoulder as she hurried down the long hallway towards the library. Heidi pushed open a panelled wood door and stepped into the room.

Shelves overflowing with leather bound books lined three walls. The fourth wall was graced by an expansive stone fireplace. A crackling fire helped to chase the chill from the room. A large mahogany desk stood in the centre of the room. It's top was piled high with papers and open books. Two chairs were pulled up to one side of the desk, inviting visitors to settle in for a long visit.

Gladys was sitting in the overstuffed office chair shuffling through papers and mumbling to herself. She was so engrossed in what she was looking for; she did not hear Heidi enter the room.

"Mom? Er...Gladys? I just talked to Molly and she said that Jansen has left. Is that true?" Heidi asked her mom, a hint of panic rising in her voice.

"Oh!" Gladys gave a start as she realised she was no longer alone. "Heidi! You scared me. I didn't hear you come in. Jansen? Oh, yes. He left right after breakfast.

Something about having to get back to work. Something pressing suddenly came up. He didn't give many details. Just that he had to get back right away."

"Did you talk to him before he left?" Heidi pressed. She paced before the desk, nervously twisting her umbrella in her hands.

"Sort of. I tried to but he seemed very distracted. It must have been something very important to have him so wound up all of a sudden."

"Do you know where Jansen lives, Gladys? Did he give his address when he checked in? I really need to talk to him." Heidi held her breath, hoping against hope that Gladys would have the information that she needed.

"I'm sorry honey. I don't know much about him. He just sort of showed up one day looking for a room for a few nights. Molly didn't get his complete address when he registered and I didn't see that information was missing until this afternoon." Gladys stood and moved towards her daughter. "Why don't you sit down for a bit? You look absolutely horrible!"

Heidi let her mom lead her to one of the leather chairs. She sank down wearily, her knees suddenly going weak. Gladys settled in the other seat. She picked up one of Heidi's hands and squeezed it gently.

"You care for Jansen, don't you?" Gladys asked softly.

"Yes," Heidi whispered. "I think I have for awhile but I wouldn't let myself. I felt that I had to be faithful to Dean. But last night I realised that I have to let Dean go and get on with my life. I came to tell Jansen that. That I am ready to let him into my life if he wants to be part of it."

"Oh, baby. I wish that there was something that I could do," Gladys said. It hurt her to see her daughter in such turmoil but knowing that Heidi was willing to give Jansen a chance now gave her hope for a brighter future. "If I had known, I could have tried to stall him longer this morning. At least until this storm set in again and then he wouldn't have been able to get out. Is there anything that I can do for you? Anything I can get you?"

Heidi shook her head. The range of emotions that she had been feeling over the past twelve hours and the disappointment of missing Jansen before he left were starting to take a toll on Heidi. "I don't think so. Unless you know of some way to magically bring Jansen back here so that I can talk to him. Even if nothing works out, at least I could tell him how I feel. It would be a first step for me to getting my life back."

"I'll talk to the staff to see if anyone knows anything about him. Maybe one of them talked to Jansen and learned something about him." Gladys suggested. She squeezed Heidi's hand a little tighter, trying to pass on silent support to her daughter.

"Oh, don't do that, Mom!" Heidi exclaimed. She looked wild eye at her mother. "I don't want anyone to know. I don't want to deal with prying questions or any more pity."

"Don't worry. I won't tell them anything about you. I'll just say that he left something behind and I want to send it to him but he left no forwarding address," Gladys quickly reassured Heidi. "Now. Why don't you go up to my room and lie down for a while. You look absolutely exhausted."

"I don't want to impose. I'll just run back to my cottage." Heidi sighed wearily. She suddenly felt deflated, as if she did not have the strength to push herself up from the chair.

"You'll do no such thing young lady! It is storming something fierce out there. That wind would blow you away in a minute," Gladys admonished her daughter lightly. She wanted to keep her close to make sure Heidi would be able to handle this new disappointment. "You just take my room. There are lots of spare beds around if you can't make it back to your own bed by tonight."

"Thanks Mom. I owe you one." Heidi pushed herself out of the chair, lightly brushed her mother's cheek with a kiss, and left the office. She wearily climbed the wide staircase up to her mother's bedroom at the top of the stairs. Exhausted, she fell onto the bed and slipped into a troubled sleep.

Gladys watched her daughter leave the room before getting up. She moved to the other side of the desk and opened a side drawer. Digging through the papers, she pulled out a small burgundy book. Flipping the pages to a note at the back, Gladys picked up the phone and dialled the number that had been written neatly on the page.

The phone rang four times before someone picked it up.

A deep male voice greeted her.

"Hello, Jansen. She really does care for you," said Gladys.

Chapter Twenty

Six months later...

Heidi nervously twisted the black leather gloves in her hands. She sat on a hard bench along the edge of a long marble hallway. People scurried up and done the hallway carrying briefcases or boxes of papers, their footsteps echoing in the silence. A woman sobbed quietly on the bench across from Heidi. Heidi felt alone even though there were dozens of people moving all around her.

"Ms. Murray?" asked a man as he approached Heidi.

Heidi looked up at the tall man standing before her. He was wearing a three-piece navy blue pinstripe suit and a crisp white shirt. The only piece that looked out of place was the colourful tie with a child's drawing on it. In his hand, the stranger carried a black leather briefcase with the initials AW engraved in gold lettering on the top left corner.

"Yes?" Heidi answered.

"Ms. Murray, I am Abe Warner, District Attorney. I am the prosecutor for the case against the men who killed your husband," introduced the man. He extended a hand out to Heidi. Heidi looked at the neatly manicured hand for a brief moment. Each fingernail was precisely cut in a tidy little square and there was no trace of dirt or grime under any of them. She reached up to shake the lawyer's hand.

"Please, call me Heidi. I hate formality."

Abe lowered himself onto the bench beside Heidi. "I just wanted to introduce myself and explain a little about what is going to happen. Today, each side is going to present their opening remarks and I will be calling my first witness. Over the next few weeks, and maybe even months, I will call witnesses to support the state's case against the defendants. Once I am done, the defence will call their witnesses to try to prove their clients' innocence. The jury will decide the verdict once everyone is done arguing. You do not need to be present during the entire trial if you do not want to be…"

"I want to be here," interrupted Heidi. "I have to be."

"I understand, Heidi. It may be a long process. And at times it will be very emotionally trying. We will be calling up memories and details that you may not want to hear or remember. Some of the medical reports are going to be very graphic and disturbing. And the defence will be trying everything they can to cast any shred of doubt on the case. They may be very brutal at times with their tactics. Do not be afraid to leave the courtroom anytime the details get to be too much. No one will hold it against you."

A head stuck out of the double doors beside the bench.

"Excuse me, Abe. But the judge is ready to start."

"That is our cue," Abe said as he rose. He held out a hand to help Heidi to her feet. "Ready?"

Heidi took a deep breath. "I think so. As ready as I will ever be."

Heidi sat in the back of the courtroom during the opening statements. From there, she had a good view of the entire proceedings. Much of the opening statements from both lawyers were lost to her as she took everything in. Her eyes were constantly drawn towards the four defendants sitting at the defence table. They were just young kids, barely in their teens. One of the kids sat huddled at the end of the table. He looked around wildly. She could see the terror in his eyes. He looked like a wild animal caught in a trap. If it had been another time, another place, different circumstances, she might have pitied him.

As the defendants rose to leave the courtroom for a short recess, one of the defendants looked back at the crowded room. He was tall and lanky with long greasy brown hair pulled back in a ponytail and secured with a brown rubber band. The orange prison jump suit hung loosely on his thin frame. There was an evil scar running across his cheek from jaw to nose. His dark eyes met Heidi's across the room.

Heidi caught her breath at what she saw. There was pure hatred in those pools of darkness. There was no soul. He leered menacingly at her, as if sending out a silent warning that she could be next. Heidi quickly averted her eyes, trying to shut out all that hatred.

Heidi slipped back into her seat in the last row as the court was called back in session. She had hardly left the courtroom during the recess, only long enough to stretch her legs for a minute. She did not want to miss a minute of the proceedings. The recess had given her a little time to think over everything that she had had heard and seen so far.

Abe Warner stood to call his first witness. "Your Honour, I would like to call my first witness. Special Agent Jansen Winfield."

Heidi started at the name. What was Jansen doing in these proceedings? And Special Agent? He owned a security company. Could there be two people with the same name? She stretched in her seat to get a better look at the witness stand. A deputy was blocking her view as he swore in the witness. She craned her neck, trying to look around the man. Finally, she was able to see Jansen. The sight took her breath away. He was dressed in a dark navy suit, a white shirt, and simple navy tie. His dark hair had been cut short. Heidi could just make out a small scar along his jaw. She could feel her heart skip a few beats at the sight of him.

Heidi shook her head. He was saying something. Something about Dean. Now was not the time to lose her head. She had to focus. Heidi turned her attention away from the handsome face on the witness stand to what he was saying. She listened as he described how he had joined an undercover operation working on breaking up a new and dangerous gang that had been moving across the country. He had spent two years in the realms of gang life, getting to know the major players and their crime patterns. Jansen described some of the common crimes associated with the gang: the robberies, the drug deals, the vandalism.

"How were new numbers recruited into the gang?" Abe asked Jansen as he paced in front of the jury, his hands clasped behind his back.

"Gang members hung around at the schools and the parks, looking for kids who needed a friend. They befriended the loners. Most of the time, they also got them hooked on drugs so that the gang would have their loyalty. The gang would supply the drugs as long as the kids did what they were told," answered Jansen.

"Was there any initiation process that went along with this recruitment?"

"Objection, Your Honour!" the defence attorney shot out of his chair in protest. He did not like where this line of questioning was heading. "What is the relevancy of this line of questioning? Does it really matter that kids tried to make friends with other kids?"

"Overruled! I think that it is important to know how this gang operated to understand the importance of the crime," said the judge before Abe could even defend his line of questioning. The judge glared at the defence attorney, silencing any further objections he may have had.

"Thank you, Your Honour," Abe replied as he cast a cocky smile at the defence table. He knew his entire argument lay in the hands of Special Agent Winfield and his testimony. This would be the most damaging bit of information that he could present. Everything else would just put the boys at the crime scene. But this bit of information would provide motive and reason. It would be their coffin. "Please continue, Special Agent Winfield."

Jansen glanced at the jury for a moment before starting his explanation. All eyes were focused on him. He had everyone's complete attention. "It would start out with a few petty crimes: breaking windows, slashing tires, harmless graffiti. Once the kids had a taste of the excitement that these crimes brought, the adrenaline rush, they would move on to bigger crimes. Ripping off the local convenience store. Break and enter. Maybe even steal a car or two. By now, the kids are really hooked on drugs and are moving into harder stuff like meth, cocaine and heroin. They are at the point of being willing to do anything for it. And committing crimes is giving them an unbelievable rush, almost as big as the drugs themselves. The final stage of the initiation is proving themselves to be absolutely loyal to the gang."

"And how is this done?" Abe asked.

"With cold-blooded murder."

Surprise and shock rippled through the audience. Even though they all knew that this was a murder trial, they did not expect it to be talked about so plainly. They had expected something more seedy and underworld-like such as a drug deal gone bad or a gang war. The judge pounded his gavel to bring everyone's attention back to the proceedings. He called everyone back to order and then nodded at Jansen to continue.

"To prove yourself absolutely loyal to the gang," Jansen continued to explain himself, "you had to be willing to kill for the gang. And not just during a gang war. You had to be willing to kill on demand and in cold blood."

"How was this first kill carried out?" asked Abe.

"It usually took the form of an early morning mugging and then stabbing the victim to death."

"It was that simple? Rob someone and then kill him?" Abe pretended surprise at the simplicity of the initiation to add a touch of drama to the proceedings. He wanted to make sure that he kept the jury's undivided attention on him and Jansen during the entire testimony.

"Not exactly," Jansen hedged. He shifted slightly in his seat. This was the crucial point in his testimony when things got very detailed and graphic. Some of the details still bothered him even. "The person had to be killed a certain way and particular things taken from the body."

Abe prodded Jansen to continue, "Can you describe the process?"

"Objection, Your Honour!" The defence lawyer jumped from his chair again. He was not liking where this was going. "I still do not see what this has to do with the case. Mr. Warner is trying to damage the jury with graphic details that are just not relevant."

"I am trying to establish the process behind how Dean Murray came to be killed while jogging in the park Sunday morning," Abe explained to the judge. "I am trying to show that it was not a simple mugging but a carefully planned murder."

"You may proceed," granted the judge. "But I will stop you if I feel that it is getting too graphic and potentially damaging to the jury."

Abe turned back to the witness stand and rephrased his question, "Special Agent Winfield, how was the victim killed?"

Heidi listened intently as Jansen described how the four boys attacked and savagely murdered their victim. She was repulsed by what she was hearing but could not make herself leave the room. Quiet sobs racked her body as she heard how the victim, and Dean, was brutalized. She shuddered as she relived the last few hours of Dean's life. It had been a life so full of promise and love. A life that had been needlessly snuffed out for someone's next score and the need to fit in. Tears coursed down Heidi's cheeks as she, once again, mourned for the man she had loved and for the future they would not get to share together. She searched the defence table for any sign of remorse, for any sign of shame for what had been done.

Many of the women in the audience broke down into sobs as Jansen continued his description. The defendant at the end of the table dropped his head as if trying to hide himself from the angry eyes that he felt boring into his back. Tears poured down his cheeks.

"Was a victim chosen at random?" Abe asked quietly. He wanted to reinforce the fact that this was all premeditated and very calculated brutality.

"No," Jansen said, shaking his head in emphasis. "An area was picked for where the crime would happen. A popular site was in the park. Then that area would be watched for a couple of months to learn people's habits. After a couple of weeks of watching, usually one person is singled out because of a consistent routine. He is watched for awhile to make sure that he doesn't vary from that routine."

"You keep referring to the victim as a he. Are only men targeted or are women also chosen?" Abe questioned with a little feigned curiosity.

"It is always a man. They offer more of a struggle and a greater thrill," Jansen confirmed. His voice held a note of contempt for the people involved in the crime.

Puzzled, Abe asked Jansen one more question, "How can two boys hold down a full grown man?"

"It is how they pin him down. He is staked down spread eagle with his wrists and ankles bound by barbed wire."

Chapter Twenty-One

Heidi waited on the hard bench outside the large double doors, watching as people streamed by. She searched the faces for signs of familiarity. Her hands nervously twisted a crumpled napkin as she waited.

The doors beside her swung open and two men walked through. They were deep in conversation and did not notice Heidi sitting along the wall.

"There is nothing that their lawyer can do to remove that ugly picture of the victim that you painted," said one of the men. Heidi immediately recognised him as the other lawyer who had been sitting at the prosecutor's table with Abe Warner. He had loosened his tie and undid the top button of his shirt. "It is an image that is going to stay with the jury for a long, long time."

"But is there enough evidence to prove that those boys were there? That they were the ones who committed the murder?" asked the other man, standing behind the lawyer out of Heidi's line of vision. "Is there any way that that weasel of a defence attorney could create doubt? Especially for Montrue. He's the one I want. He's the mastermind. But his prescence is the one that's most shady at the crime scene."

Heidi immediately recognised the deep voice of the other man before she could clearly see him. It was her hero, her angel.

Jansen glanced over his companion's shoulder and noticed a white faced Heidi staring at them. "Heidi!" exclaimed Jansen. He moved around the other man to sit on the bench beside her. "What are you doing here?"

"I had to come," Heidi said in a quiet voice. She looked down at her hands. "I had to see the monsters who did this. I have to see them pay."

"I'm so sorry that you had to hear everything today. Someone should have warned you. Someone should have taken you out of the courtroom," Jansen said. He picked up one of Heidi's hands and held it tightly in his own. It was cold and clammy from tension. Jansen tried to pass some of his warmth through to Heidi as he squeezed her hand.

"No. I have to be here. I have to hear everything," Heidi insisted. Her voice cracked slightly under the strain of the day's proceedings. She suddenly felt very weary.

The man who had left the courtroom with Jansen cleared his throat and said, "Jansen, I will catch up with you later. We can talk about your cross-examination tomorrow morning before court resumes."

Jansen looked up at the other man, a silent thank you filling his eyes. "Okay. Thanks John. I'll see you at seven."

After John had moved off down the hall, Jansen turned to Heidi and tenderly took both her hands in his. He searched her eyes before asking, "Are you okay?"

Heidi took a deep breath, letting it out slowly. She said, "I'm surviving."

"Why don't we get out of here and go someplace a little more relaxing?" Jansen suggested as he gently pulled Heidi to her feet. He led her from the courthouse to a navy blue, government-issued sedan.

Jansen poured more wine into Heidi's glass before settling on the couch beside her. He stretched his arm out along the back of the couch, gently brushing against Heidi's shoulders. Heidi leaned her head back against his arm.

"How are you doing now?" asked Jansen.

"Better," said Heidi. "Though it has definitely been an emotional day."

"You shouldn't have come alone." Jansen swirled the wine in his glass as he tried to control the riot of emotions he was feeling. So much had happened in the past few months. He wanted to tell Heidi everything but did not know where to start. "Where is your mother? Why didn't she come with you?"

"She's busy looking after the inn," Heidi answered. She leaned forward and gently placed her wine glass on the glass coffee table in front of her. Then she settled back on the soft cushions, tucking her legs underneath her. "And she's not one to give much support. She's not really a touchy-feely sort of person. Anyway, I wouldn't want her to know what all happened to Dean. It would tarnish her picture of the happy world we all live in."

"And what about you?" Jansen asked, concern filling his voice. The strength Heidi was showing continued to amaze him. He did not know if he would be holding up so well if one of his loved ones had died in such a brutal way. "Don't you think it would be better not to know all the details. To just remember the good times without being reminded of the end?"

"I have to know. I have to know that Dean's death will not go unjustified," Heidi said with all the conviction she could muster. She nervously tugged at some lint on her tan slacks.

Jansen played idly with a lock of Heidi's hair. Her bravery and gumption made him proud. Tiny strings pulled at Jansen's heart. He had an overwhelming desire to wrap his arms around Heidi and not let go until this ugly trial was over.

"My heart stopped beating for a minute when I saw you on that stand," said Heidi. "You were the last person I expected to see today."

"I'm sorry about that. I wanted to tell you who I was, what I did a hundred times. But I was scared to. I didn't know how you would react."

"Did you know that I was living at Hadey's Cove when you came up?"

Jansen leaned forward on the couch, resting his elbows on his knees. He studied a spot on the carpet while he tried to formulate an answer in his mind. He knew he had to tell Heidi the truth, no matter what happened. "Yes. I needed to get out of town for a while. My cover was getting shaky with the gang and I had to disappear for a while to protect the case. And myself. I went up to Hadey's Cove to see how you were doing. To see if you were okay. And to see if you were safe."

"Is that the only reason you spent time with me?" Heidi turned to study Jansen. A heavy weight settled in the pit of her stomach. She held her breath while she waited for Jansen's answer.

"Oh, Heidi! Don't ever think that!" said Jansen. He took both of her hands in his. "I wanted to get to know you. That first day you walked into the dining room, I was drawn to you. I couldn't keep my eyes off you. All my senses were filled with you. And the more time that I spent with you, the more you became a part of me. It got to the point that I just couldn't stay away. No matter how much it hurt. I desperately wanted to hold you, to cover your body in kisses, to make love to you. But I didn't want to rush you. I knew what you had gone through."

Heidi laid her hand on Jansen's cheek and lightly rubbed her thumb against his soft skin. She could feel a few whiskers that had already sprouted along his jaw line.

"Why, Jansen?" she whispered, self doubt edging her voice. "Why would you want to do all that to me?"

"Because I love you."

The words came out sounding strangled, but Jansen knew he had to say them. This might not be the way that he imagined telling her that he wanted to spend the rest of his life with her, but he needed to say the words to make her understand. He had been attracted to the woman the first time he had seen her while undercover. He had fallen in love with her the second he had seen her at Hadey's Cove.

Jansen leaned toward Heidi and looked deep into her eyes. He searched their depths for a sign that his love was not unwelcome. What he saw filled him with hope. He was not too late. He would still have a chance to explain everything.

"I had been part of the gang for about six months when Dean was attacked," Jansen explained. He reached over and gently took one of Heidi's hands into his own. Her hand trembled slightly in his. Squeezing slightly, Jansen tried to reassure Heidi that everything would be okay.

"I had heard some rumblings about an attack being planned but by the time I got enough details to know what was happening, it was too late. Dean was already gone." Jansen heaved a deep breath. A lump formed at the back of his throat, making it difficult to talk. He rubbed a hand roughly over his face, trying to forget what he saw that day.

"All I could do was take a few pictures of the guys responsible and try to get the police there before they got too far away.

I couldn't even do that though. They had a car stashed about a block from the park. They got away before anyone else could see them. I had seen the car, too, and knew that something was wrong with it. It just wasn't in the right place for someone to be visiting the park. I should have followed my gut and disabled it. Then the cops would have been able to catch the perps and have enough evidence to put them away for life no questions asked."

Guilt still haunted Jansen over that day. There were so many if-onlys—if only he had disabled the getaway car, if only he had gotten to the park fifteen minutes sooner, if only he had been smart enough to figure out the plan sooner. But no amount of if-onlys would ever change the past. He had learned to deal with that before but he had never quite gotten over blaming himself when anything went wrong.

Heidi sat quietly through Jansen's confession. Tears coursed down her cheeks. She had not been the only one to suffer from the loss of Dean. She had lost her husband, a man she had loved with all her heart. Jansen had lost a little bit of confidence in his ability to do his job without error, to protect society.

She looked down at the hand that held her own. It was so strong, yet at the same time, so gentle. How could she not love this man? A man who gave away a little chunk of his life to bring peace to hers.

"You have brought justice down on the people who hurt Dean," Heidi said, her voice barely a whisper. She took a steadying breath, willing herself to be strong so she that she could tell Jansen how much what he did meant to her. "And you saved many more people from dying such a brutal death. Dean's death will not be for nothing when those murderers go to jail.

I will never be able to repay you for everything that you have done for me. You may not have been able to save Dean but you did save me. You gave me my life back and showed me that I can love again."

Jansen raised his bent head and turned towards Heidi. Amazement crept in to slowly replace little of the pain clouding his eyes as the full extent of Heidi's words sank in. Sitting beside him was an incredible woman. Even after he admitted seeing Dean's murder take place and not being able to do anything to save him, Heidi could still see him as a hero.

"You are such an amazing woman," Jansen said. He pulled Heidi closer so he could cup her face in his hands. Gently, he caressed her soft cheeks with the pad of his thumbs. "I do not deserve your gratitude."

"You deserve so much more Jansen. Do not ever sell yourself short," Heidi said vehemently. She wrapped her arms around Jansen's neck and laid her forehead against his. "Your heart is pure gold Jansen. There is nothing that you would not do for someone else. No matter the cost to you. It is me that does not deserve you or the love that you have to offer."

Jansen's throat was thick with emotion. Everything he had ever dreamed of rested in the palm of his hand. There was so much he wanted to say but the words were stuck in his throat. He managed to whisper in a husky voice, "You deserve the world, darling."

Heidi laid her lips tenderly against Jansen, pouring out the depths of her soul in that gentle touch. It spoke of the deep love she was filled with for the man she held in her arms. It spoke of her future. Of their future. A bright future full of promise and hope.

Jansen responded with equal emotion. He pulled Heidi onto his lap in a desperate attempt to bring her even closer. He buried his hands in her silken tresses as he deepened the kiss. He tilted Heidi's head slightly for better access to her sensuous mouth.

Tender kisses became more fervent as desire took over. Hands fumbled with buttons in a desperate attempt to expose skin. Pants followed shirts as clothes were shed and discarded without a second thought.

Jansen laid Heidi down on a plush fleece blanket he had spread out in front of the fireplace. The light from the fire flickered and danced across Heidi's skin. Jansen paused a moment to drink in Heidi's beauty before following the light with a trail of kisses.

Few words exchanged, few were needed, as Heidi and Jansen explored each other's bodies. They used their hands, their mouths, and their tongues to say all that they were feeling. When they finally came together, it was an intense and powerful joining. Two souls became one.

Afterwards, Jansen pulled Heidi tight against him. He never wanted to let go of this incredible woman. Only in his wildest dreams had he ever thought that he would be so lucky to find such soul-binding love.

Heidi snuggled up against Jansen's shoulder and breathed deeply. A sense of peace washed over her. For the first time in a long while, Heidi was not afraid to close her eyes.

Chapter Twenty-Two

Morning sunlight streamed through the open window, warming Heidi with its heat. For a moment, the strange bed startled Heidi. Slowly, memories of the night before filtered through the fogginess as Heidi began to wake up. She stretched languidly, a smile spreading across her face. She burrowed deeper under the goose down duvet and breathed in deeply the scent of the man she loved with all her being.

Sometime during the night, Jansen had carried Heidi to his bed and showed her all over again how much he loved her. Their joining had been tender and full of promise. Promise of a future together.

Heidi sighed a happy sigh. For the first time in a long time, she felt content right down to the tips of her toes. She was eager to face the day instead of dreading it. Peace now filled the empty hollows of her soul that had been left behind by Dean's murder.

On the pillow beside her, Jansen had laid a handful of pansies on top of a note. Heidi breathed in the fresh scent of the flowers as she opened the note. She smiled at the bold, sprawling handwriting. It was so much like the man who wrote it—strong and powerful yet tender and gentle at the same time.

"My love," Heidi read the note out loud, "I had to run out for a quick minute. Stay in bed and rest and I'll feed you a breakfast fit for the queen you truly are. Love, Jansen."

Heidi snuggled back among the pillows. After a long, emotional journey, she was finally back where she belonged. She was in love with a wonderful man and she was ready to move forward with her life.

Energised with the thoughts of new opportunities, Heidi threw off the covers and jumped out of bed. To the room around her, Heidi said, "Jansen's already done so much for me. It's time that I started doing something for him. And the least I can do is have a big breakfast ready for him when he gets back. Or a big pot of coffee anyway."

Heidi whistled a jaunty tune, only slightly off-key, as she padded towards the bathroom. It was every woman's dream bathroom. A granite vanity with deep, double sinks stretched along one wall. A gilded, antique mirror rested against the vanity and was flanked by brush nickel wall sconces. Nestled in the nook created by a floor-to-ceiling bay window was a jetted bathtub large enough to easily accommodate two people and whatever activities they might want to partake in.

Heidi gazed longingly at the elegant tub. She could really enjoy stretching out in a tubful of bubbles right now. But that would have to wait for another time. Maybe tonight when Jansen would be home to join her. With a soft sigh, Heidi turned from the tub towards a shower the size of her entire bathroom in her cottage.

Heidi adjusted the water to the perfect temperature and stepped into the tiled shower. Water streamed down at her from six strategically placed showerheads. The water felt like six highly skilled masseuses kneading and caressing Heidi's muscles into supplication.

"Mmm...pure heaven," sighed Heidi. She reached for the shampoo bottle sitting on a ledge in the corner and squeezed a generous dollop onto the palm of her hand. Heidi vigorously rubbed the shampoo into her hair. Turning around, she stepped back under the stream of water and rinsed the suds out.

Heidi reached for a bath towel hanging from a hook on the wall as she stepped out of the shower. She dried the water from her body and then wrapped the towel around her head turban-style to slow the rivulet of water running down her back from her hair.

Returning to the bedroom, Heidi looked around for her clothes. There seemed to be no hide nor hair of her clothes anywhere.

"Everything must still be in the livingroom where we left it last night," Heidi said aloud to the empty room. An involuntary shiver trickled down her back. Everything felt so still, as if frozen in time. Heidi mentally shook herself. It was just the strangeness of being in a man's home again and all by herself. "Maybe Jansen has something I can borrow until I get my clothes so the neighbours don't get too much of a show."

Heidi opened a panelled door across from the foot of the bed and found a neat row of clothes hanging inside. She pulled out a blue and white hockey jersey with the name of a neighbourhood rec centre team emblazoned on the front and Coach stamped on the back. She pulled it over her head. Heidi had always enjoyed wearing guys' jerseys. She could see herself wearing this particular jersey on future Saturday mornings as she enjoyed breakfast with the man she loved.

Heidi hugged herself close. She could hardly wait for Jansen to come back so she could see him again. So she could talk to him again. So she could start her future.

As Heidi padded through the livingroom towards the kitchen, the sound of the doorbell broke through the silence. The eerie shiver that had rippled down Heidi's spine when she first woke up returned with a vengeance.

"It's not happening again. It's not," Heidi whispered. She stopped in the middle of the room and held her breath, waiting. The doorbell rang again. "It can't."

In a trance, Heidi moved to the landing area between the living room and kitchen. Her hand shook as she reached out to turn the knob. As the door swung open, Heidi saw a blue uniform. She grabbed at the doorjamb to save herself from falling. All the blood had drained from her head and the breath caught in her throat.

"Good morning, ma'am," the blue uniform said in a

bright, friendly voice. "I have a delivery for Mr. Jansen Winfield. I just need a signature on the bottom line."

Heidi's eyes slowly focused as the words began to sink in. The man standing in front of her was not a police officer coming to tell her that something terrible had happened to Jansen. It was not the same as that morning only a couple of years ago. No. This time it was only a messenger and everything was still right in Heidi's world. Jansen was still coming home to her. Relief flooded threw Heidi in great waves until she was almost giddy with it.

The messenger politely cleared his throat and gestured with a raised eyebrow towards the clipboard he was holding out to Heidi. Heidi quickly reached for the clipboard and pen. She scribbled her name on the line indicated. Exchanging the clipboard for a thick manila envelope, Heidi mumbled a thank you and have a good day before closing the door. She leaned against the solid wood door and gulped in large lungfuls of air.

When she finally got her breathing under control, Heidi looked down at the package she clutched in her hands. Scrawled across it in red block letters were the words: IMPORTANT DOCUMENTS—TO BE OPENED BY ADDRESSEE ONLY. Underneath that was Jansen's name and address. Heidi looked at the address label in the top left hand corner. The package was from Hadey's Cove Realty.

"What could Doris be sending Jansen?" Heidi wondered aloud. "I can't think of any reason a Special Agent would have business with Hadey's Cove Realty. It's not really the sort of place to be involved with any criminal activities."

Heidi shrugged her shoulders. Jansen would be home soon. Maybe he would explain it all to her then. She was not in the position yet to be demanding answers or opening mail. She would just have to be patient and wait for Jansen to fill her in. If it was anything important. It might be nothing at all. She would not worry about it right now. She had more important things to think about. Like making coffee.

Heidi placed the envelope on the entrance way table before moving into the kitchen. She grabbed the coffee pot and filled it with cold water. Humming a song only slightly out of tune, Heidi searched the cupboards above the coffeemaker for coffee.

Because of all the banging she was making looking for coffee grounds, Heidi did not hear the front door open. She did not hear Jansen come in. He stood in the entrance way of the kitchen, watching Heidi sashay around the tiny space.

"A man could get used to a sight like this in his kitchen," Jansen said, announcing his presence.

Heidi gave a start at the unexpected voice. She swore loudly when the can of coffee slipped from her hands and landed on her bare foot.

Jansen stepped into the kitchen to assess the damage his appearance had caused. "Oh, baby. I didn't mean to startle you."

"I didn't hear you come in," explained Heidi. "I thought that I was still alone."

"You were banging around pretty good when I walked in the door. You probably couldn't hear me. In fact," Jansen moved closer to Heidi, invading her space so that she was forced to take a step back. He matched Heidi step for step until he backed her into the counter. He leaned forward, pinning Heidi with his body. "There was so much noise in here I thought someone had broken in and was robbing me. I was all ready to come charging in here and demand justice."

"And what, may I ask, would you do to demand justice?" Heidi asked. She rubbed playfully up against Jansen's hard body. His reaction was immediate and very evident. Heidi could feel the bulge pressing against her stomach. She wiggled again and her body responded in kind. Heat pooled and nipples hardened in anticipation.

"First, I would have grabbed the intruder's arms and pinned them behind his back like this." Jansen circled each of Heidi's wrists and pulled her arms back behind her. "And then I would do this."

Jansen bent his head down and nibbled along Heidi's jawbone. He continued nipping along the sensitive skin of Heidi's neck. Slowly, he feathered kisses along Heidi's collarbone and back up the other side of her neck. She fairly quivered with pleasure.

Shifting his grip on Heidi's wrists so only one hand held them, Jansen used his now free hand to pull the jersey up.

He pulled the shirt up over Heidi's head, trapping her arms in its folds so he could free his other hand.

Jansen bent his head to trail kisses across the top of Heidi's breasts as his hands skimmed over the smooth skin of her stomach. His tongue circled a nipple. Heidi's breath quickened as pleasure flowed through her veins. A soft moan escaped her lips as Jansen teased and tugged her hardened nipples.

Jansen grasped Heidi around her hips and gently lifted her onto the counter. He nudged her thighs apart so he could step between them. Heidi wrapped her legs around Jansen's waist and pulled him closer. She snuggled up against him, trying to get closer. Jansen ran his hands lightly up Heidi's thighs, sending shivers racing down her back. His fingers brushed against the junction of her thighs. He could feel the heat his attentions were generating through the silky fabric of her panties. He slipped one finger beneath the fabric.

Heidi gasped as Jansen tangled his fingers in her delicate hairs. The back of his knuckles brushed against her feminine folds, sending another round of shivers rushing through her. Slowly, Jansen eased a finger between the soft folds and into the core of Heidi's heat. Heidi's muscles contracted slightly to grip Jansen's finger. With slow, deliberate movements, Jansen slid his finger in and out. Heidi's pulse quickened and her breath caught in her throat.

Jansen returned his mouth to Heidi's and trapped the

low moan that rumbled in her throat with a deep, heated kiss. He melded his lips against hers. Dipping his tongue into Heidi's mouth, Jansen explored the moist depths. His tongue twined with hers in a playful game of passion.

Heidi's world narrowed done to one fine point, centred around the intense sensations Jansen was evoking with his finger. Her breath came in ragged pants as wave upon wave of desire crashed against her heart. She could feel the point of no return rushing at her full speed.

As if sensing how close Heidi was to reaching her peak, Jansen quickly wriggled out of his dark denim jeans and entered her in one smooth motion. His movements were slow and slightly restrained. No matter how overcome with passion he was, Jansen wanted to take everything slow with the goddess in front of him. Everything right down to making love for hours. His own pleasure would be from making Heidi happy again.

Heidi arched backwards to accept the full length of Jansen into her. Fireworks were exploding behind her eyes. She did not want the feelings to end but her climax was on a crash course to peaking and there was nothing she could do to slow it. All conscious thought drained from Heidi's head as Jansen shifted, changing the pressure between Heidi's legs. She could only gasp as her muscles spasmed and the fireworks turned into a kaleidoscope of colour.

He tried to hold back, to give Heidi all the pleasure, but Jansen's climax came swiftly on the waves of Heidi's. They clung to each other as their heartbeats slowed and their ragged breaths returned to normal.

"Wow," breathed Heidi. "I think I should break into your house more often. You really now how to punish an intruder."

Jansen pushed a stray lock of hair out of Heidi's face before kissing her gently on the mouth. "Only when they look as gorgeous as you do I pull out all the stops. I don't think this jersey has ever looked so good."

Heidi wiggled on the counter, trying to free her arms so she could wrap them around the man in front of her. Jansen reached behind her back and pulled the sweater free of her arms. "Ummm...that's better," murmured Heidi as she slid her hands up Jansen's chest. His muscles quivered under her roving fingers.

Jansen stilled Heidi's hands with his own as they moved up to playfully rub his nipples. He brought each hand to his lips, gently brushing a kiss across the knuckles. "As much as I would love to discipline you more for leaving the bedroom, I really need to get some food into me. You plum wore me out last night."

"I was just making you some coffee when you so rudely interrupted me." Heidi indicated the coffee pot beside her with a nod of her head. "If you would be so kind as to let me down, I can finish doing what I started."

Jansen chucked Heidi under the chin before helping her off the counter. As she turned to retrieve the jersey from behind her, he swatted her gently on the bottom. "I was going to make you breakfast and feed you in bed. And then maybe feast on you myself after."

"I know but I couldn't sleep anymore and I wanted to do something for you," Heidi said. She placed the coffee pot back into the coffee maker and pressed start. Within seconds, coffee began to drip down into the pot and the fragrant aroma of brewing coffee filled the kitchen.

"Hmmm... You were planning on making breakfast?" Jansen asked. He wrapped his arms around Heidi and nuzzled her bare neck. "But I thought you couldn't even boil water?"

Heidi snuggled back against Jansen. She tilted her head to allow Jansen better access to the delicate skin of her neck. "No, but I can manage to make coffee. I thought I could at least have that ready for you. And show you that I'm not completely helpless. Besides, coffee is what got me through college so I had to learn quickly how to make it."

"Well, I was thinking of making French toast with fresh fruit and whipped cream. How does that sound?" Jansen asked.

"Divine," answered Heidi. She turned in Jansen's arms so she could better return some of the pleasure that his nibbles were giving her. She reached up on tiptoes to nibble along his stubble-roughened jaw line. "Of course, not as good as you but a definite close second."

"Well, little missy, if that suits you, then that is what breakfast will be. But you are going to have to leave the kitchen or I will never get anything made. Why don't you go into the living room and find some cartoons or something and I'll serve you breakfast on the couch."

Jansen stepped back to free Heidi from his trap. With one last peck on the cheek, Heidi left Jansen in the kitchen to work his magic. She padded into the living room and settled on the long couch facing the big screen television. She reached for the remote to find something to entertain herself while Jansen slaved away in the kitchen. Within minutes, Heidi found an old black and white movie and had curled up to watch it. It was not long before her eyes grew heavy and she dozed off.

When Jansen walked into the living room to bring breakfast to Heidi, he found her curled into a ball, snoring softly. He set the plate of French toast on the coffee table and sat down beside it. There was something peaceful about watching a woman sleep. Jansen wanted to soak up as much of it as possible before Heidi woke up.

Chapter Twenty-Three

The sun was just starting to dip behind the tall buildings of downtown, painting the sky brilliant shades of reds, oranges, pinks, and purples. Heidi spread the morning paper out in front of her on the glass top table. She had come out onto the small patio off the living room to enjoy the warm evening and to wait for Jansen to finish making dinner. She curled up on the soft cushion of the patio chair and reached for the glass of wine she had placed on the table in front of her.

It had been a busy day. After a delicious breakfast of French toast and fresh fruit, Heidi and Jansen had went together to the courthouse to listen to another day of testimony. There had not been much progress made in the case. Just a lot of arguing between the crown and defence about what evidence could and could not be allowed. It had been very draining for Heidi. And very frustrating. She was eager to see justice served.

When they had left the courthouse after a long afternoon of bickering, Jansen had suggested a quiet dinner in. He promised to make a meal that would make

Heidi forget all her worries. Heidi jumped at the chance to return home with Jansen. His house was so much more appealing than spending a lonely evening in her hotel room with only her thoughts to keep her company.

Now, Heidi was relaxing on the patio with a mellow glass of wine and the daily paper while Jansen banged around in the kitchen. She flipped through the newsprint until she came to the classified section.

"Looking for anything particular or just browsing?" asked Jansen as he leaned down to place a kiss on the top of Heidi's head. He placed the tray of chicken breasts he was carrying on the table and turned towards the grill in the corner of the patio. Turning a few knobs, he soon had the grill lighted and ready for the chicken.

Heidi watched Jansen as he moved around the corner. She loved the play of muscles under the dark material of his shirt as he reached and stretched. The worn denim of his jeans hugged the rippling muscles of his long, lean legs and rounded buttocks. It was a sight Heidi would never grow tired of. Heidi shook herself out of her daydream to answer Jansen, "I just thought I would take a look and see what apartments are available."

"Moving are you?" Jansen pulled out the chair beside Heidi and sat down. He reached for the other glass of wine on the table and took a drink. "Find anything interesting?"

"Nothing in my price range or in a safe area of the city," said Heidi. She carefully folded up the newspaper and set it aside. "I was thinking it was maybe time to move back.

The city holds some attraction again."

"Yes. There are some great new shops opening up. And the zoo has a new pair of lions," Jansen said, a teasing note to his voice. He winked playfully at Heidi.

Heidi picked up her wineglass, cradling the thin crystal bowl in her hands. She needed something to hide the slight tremor in her hands. Jansen was not going to make this easy. It had been so long that she had to talk about her feelings with a man. Since high school, Dean had known how she felt about it. And there had never been anyone else to ignited even close to the same level of feeling in her as Jansen. She took a sip of wine, hoping for a little courage from the bubbly liquid. She tried to adopt the same light note as Jansen. "Well, as nice as lions are, they really don't hold much attraction for me. There's something a little less hairy that I'm thinking about."

Jansen chuckled at Heidi as a rosy shade spread across her pale cheeks. A blushing woman had always intrigued Jansen and Heidi was definitely no exception. He stood up from the table and took a peek at the chicken on the grill. "Hold that thought, darling. Let me go get the rest of dinner and we'll continue this very interesting conversation. I am eager to hear what attracts you more than a hairy lion."

As soon as Jansen was back in the house and out of eyesight, Heidi buried her head in her hands. This was a lot harder than she ever remembered. Of course, Jansen was not making it any easier on her. But how does someone go about telling someone else that she is ready to start living again and is thinking of moving to the same city as him because she does not want to be too far away? Heidi did not want to rush things but she definitely wanted to spend a lot more time with Jansen. She just could not do that while living in Hadey's Cove. It was time to return to this city and be with the man she loved.

Jansen pushed open the screen door with his toe. His arms were laden down with trays of steaming food and dishes. Heidi jumped up to relieve him of a few pieces before something landed on the ground. "Here let me help you with something. Ummm... Something smells absolutely divine."

"Thanks. I thought I could get it all in one trip," Jansen said. He placed the remaining dishes on the table, arranging them carefully around the two place settings. "But there was a little more than I calculated. Sit down and dig in. Can you see anything I might have missed?"

"I think you have everything. There's more than enough food here anyway. I'm sure we won't realise it even if you did miss anything," said Heidi. She did not know where to start. Everything looked and smelled delicious.

"While you dig in, I have something I want to talk to you about." Jansen passed Heidi the plate of chicken. "I know you had started talking about moving back to the city before I went in but I wanted to discuss something before you went too far."

Jansen removed a manila envelope from his back

pocket and placed it on the table beside him. "You know that this letter was delivered this morning. And that I had left early to do some errands. Well, those errands were related to what's in this envelope."

Heidi's curiosity was sparked. She remembered that the return address on the envelope was stamped with a Hadey's Cove Realty watermark. Again, she wondered what business Jansen had with the realtor in her hometown.

Jansen reached across the table to take Heidi's hand in his. He lazily rubbed his thumb across the delicate skin on the back of her hand. "When you took me on a tour of Hadey's Cove, I fell in love with the town. It is exactly the type of place that I had always imagined settling down in and starting a family. I told you over ice cream that I had always wanted to own a small town hardware store. When Doris told us that Henry was selling his store, I started to get an idea. Hadey's Cove was everything I wanted in a place to live and the store provided me with the perfect opportunity to start my own business. And of course, there was one other bonus in the town."

Jansen smiled shyly at Heidi. He paused for a moment to study her reaction to his story. Seeing only a positive response so far, he continued. "Since I came back to the city, I have been talking with Doris about buying the hardware store. We finally closed the deal last week. In this envelope are the papers of ownership. You are now looking at the proud owner of Henry's Hardware.

"This morning I was meeting with another realtor to sign the papers for the sale of this place. As of two weeks from now, I will be officially homeless. So, to get to the point of this long winded story, there is something I want to ask you. I know that we are only starting to explore our feelings for each other. And there is a long road ahead of us but I know one thing for sure. I want to spend the rest of my life with you. I want to grow old with you at my side. But I also don't want to rush you or push you into something you are not ready for.

"What I am trying to say is can I move to Hadey's Cove to be near you and to grow our relationship? Would you still be willing to see me and see where life takes us?"

Jansen looked at Heidi, pleading with his eyes to say yes. His mouth was tense as he waited for Heidi to answer. Unconsciously, his grip on Heidi's hand had tightened throughout his story until he was clinging to it like a lifeline. In a way, it was a lifeline to him. Heidi represented a chance to have the life and the family that he had always dreamed about.

Heidi searched Jansen's eyes and face for a moment before answering. She saw all the love he had for her reflected in his features. There was also a vulnerability that she had not expected. Jansen always seemed so strong and sure. Like nothing could ever get him down. Now she could see that he was just as scared about the future as she was.

"Oh, Jansen. I would love for you to come and live in

Hadey's Cove. I want a future with you, too. I was going to move back to the city just to be near you, even though this place holds too many painful memories."

Jansen let out the breath that he did not know he was holding in one long whoosh. Relief spread through him. He knew that he could be rushing Heidi by talking about moving closer to her so soon after declaring his love but he could not contain his excitement any longer. He had been waiting all day to tell her the good news. He had wanted the moment to be just right, a moment that they would remember in future years when they were old and greying. "You are such a special person, Heidi. I don't know what I have ever done to deserve you. I only hope that I can live up to you. That I can make you happy. You deserve the world and I want to give that to you."

"Jansen there is nothing that you could do to make you any less of a terrific person than you already are." Heidi reached across the table to take Jansen's other hand in hers. She squeezed tightly, trying to show all her emotions through one simple touch. "You have already given me so much. You have given me my life back. My future. I am the one who doesn't deserve you and all that you have to give."

Jansen sat quietly watching Heidi for a minute. A soft chuckle rumbled up from deep within his chest. "This may be our first fight—who deserves who more. If this is what all our fights are going to be like, we are going to have one very promising, long life together."

"I wouldn't want it any other way."

Pushing his chair back from the table, Jansen tugged gently on Heidi's hand until she rose from her own chair. He pulled her onto his lap and into his arms. A stray wisp of hair fell across Heidi's pale cheek. Jansen brushed the strand back, tucking it behind her ear. He twined his fingers in the curls that tumbled along the length of her neck.

"You are so beautiful," whispered Jansen. He pulled Heidi close against his chest, wrapping his arms tight around her. "I want to hold you in my arms and never let go. I love you so much it almost hurts."

"Dean was my first love. The love of my life. But through his death, I've learned that love can give you second chances. Thank you for being my second chance."

Heidi leaned forward to press her lips against Jansen's, pouring her heart and soul into that one kiss. In the distance, the night song of an unknown bird could be heard.

Also available from PublishAmerica

MASON-DIXON MURDERS
by Bob Walsh

Heather Macy returns home to become a partner in her father's law firm in a city in southern Pennsylvania. Macy House is in a village across the Mason-Dixon Line in Maryland. Heather's father, W. Henry Macy, inherited the "General's Farm" in 1973. The M-D Line happens to run through it. Heather encounters two simultaneous murder investigations. The murders, separated by 30 years, were committed on the same spot, but the bodies were buried on opposite sides of the border. Heather meets a hermit who has been keeping a record for 30 years of visiting car license plates. He started the "diary" after the first murder. The DNA that the Pennsylvania police gather matches the remains in the Maryland case. Heather unravels the DNA connection and locates both murder weapons. Henry's twin brother Arthur writes a deathbed letter identifying whom he believes committed the 1973 murder. Some arrests are made. One testimony triggers a series of conspiracy confessions by others. One of the 2003 license plate numbers is an accurate but misleading clue.

Paperback, 378 pages
6" x 9"
ISBN 1-4137-8679-0

About the author:

Bob Walsh was born in Melfort, Sask. He graduated from the Royal Military College as a pilot, and followed that with work in finance and then as a senior administrator in the public service, retiring in 1995. Bob married Colette Boisvert from Sherbrooke, Quebec. They have three children and five grandchildren, all living near them in Ottawa. Bob's hobbies include curling and woodworking. Retirement has allowed him to work on several inventions and write fiction.

Available to all bookstores nationwide.
www.publishamerica.com

Also available from PublishAmerica

THE END OF SUMMER
by J. Nolting

The End of Summer is a provocative novel filled with excitement, yet it possesses warmth as congenial as a little old lady with frail fingers, adjusting her red hat and admiring the beautiful autumn countryside of the Midwest from the bus as it passes by her...

Amber, a teenage runaway, gets in all kinds of trouble in the red light district of New York City as she seeks fame and fortune as a professional dancer. On her way back home after five years presumed dead, she makes friends with a little old lady, who relates to her that when she was young, she also had a tumultuous past as an Army nurse in WWII.

The two become close friends and exchange the stories of their pasts.

Paperback, 190 pages
6" x 9"
ISBN 1-4241-3803-5

About the author:

J. Nolting resides in Cedar Falls with her husband. She has two grown children who live out of state. She attended the University of Iowa's writer's summer workshop, the Hearst Center for the Arts, and Hawkeye Community College. In the summers, she tours Iowa and parts of the Midwest on her motorcycle, getting inspiration for her novels. Currently she is working on a third novel.

Available to all bookstores nationwide.
www.publishamerica.com

Also available from PublishAmerica

WEREWOLF ISLAND
by Tony Gardner

Werewolf Island is Tony Gardner's breakthrough novel. He has gained his extraordinary sense of the macabre through his experience running his own haunted attraction. When he is not writing or working, he enjoys flying, scuba diving, fishing, boating and martial arts.

Paperback, 180 pages
5.5" x 8.5"
ISBN 1-4241-6995-X

About the author:

Werewolf Island is Tony Gardner's breakthrough novel. He has gained his extraordinary sense of the macabre through his experience running his own haunted attraction. When he is not writing or working, he enjoys flying, scuba diving, fishing, boating and martial arts.

Available to all bookstores nationwide.
www.publishamerica.com

Also available from PublishAmerica

LORI, RUNAWAY WIFE

by Valentine Dmitriev

Pretty, young Lori Becker is a nursing intern at a Queens hospital and is a battered wife. Professionally skilled, she is socially naïve. Intimidated by her brutal husband, Lori lives in the fantasy world of romance mysteries, idolizing their handsome author, Ian Damion.

A car accident sends Francine Ross, an unmarried, pregnant woman to the maternity ward where Lori works. The distraught man accompanying Francine is Ian Damion. Francine's full-term infant is delivered. Her casual liaison with Ian is over, and she grants him custody of his newborn son. Ian must return to Washington State. He needs a baby's nanny. Concealing her identity, Lori volunteers. This is her chance to escape from her husband. Lori matures, develops self-esteem and falls in love with Ian, but when he returns her love and proposes, Lori must confess that she's a married woman.

Paperback, 229 pages
6" x 9"
ISBN 1-60672-173-9

About the author:

Valentine Dmitriev has a Ph.D in early childhood education and has published professional articles and nine fiction and nonfiction books. Retired from the University of Washington Dr. Dmitriev lives in a retirement community near Hackettstown, New Jersey. A widow, she's the mother of a daughter and two sons.

Available to all bookstores nationwide.
www.publishamerica.com

Also available from PublishAmerica

BACKNTIME
by K. Carson Kirk

Wayne "Poor Boy" Burke was the electrician at the coal mine. His world was turned upside down when he received a letter from the love of his life informing him that she was pregnant by another man. This literally put him on a dirt floor. With help from his former boss, he rose to respectability, only to make a second mistake in his choice of a mate.

Julia wrongfully divorced her husband, Brad, the father of her children. He joined the army in World War Two and lost his life in the Battle of the Bulge.

"She took everything," he once confided to his foxhole buddy, "the house, the truck, my three kids, and damned near my life 'cause I almost pulled the trigger a couple of times."

A Scotchman, William "Warp" Broderick fled to Australia after World War One to escape his past, but it caught up with him and ended tragically.

Paperback, 475 pages
6" x 9"
ISBN 1-4241-1159-5

About the author:

K. Carson Kirk has a talent for storytelling and use of words. In this book he goes back to the 1940s, during and after World War Two, picking up the lives of many in the southwest Virginia mining area as they struggled to get on with their lives after the war ended and the big mining companies closed, leaving many out of work and literally scattering its people all over the United States and as far away as Australia.

Available to all bookstores nationwide.
www.publishamerica.com

Also available from PublishAmerica

A Nanosecond to Eternity in the Twinkling of an Eye

by Donald L. Montgomery

IS THERE A HEAVEN IN OUR FUTURE? The Bible has many references to Heaven, especially in Revelations. Here, John describes Heaven at great length; the immense size of it and the breathtaking beauty of the exterior radiance, like a most rare jewel, like a jasper, clear as crystal. Bob Tyler, the main character in this story, tells us about meeting his guardian angel, Thomas. Through Thomas, Bob meets his now deceased, earthly family and all of them are given a grand tour of Heaven with all of its grandeur, interesting places to see, great places to dine, and exciting things to do. Thomas also shows the horrendous future that will befall the inhabitants of Earth on a television screen. He shows them how God destroyed the earth, in a ball of fire, and then restored our planet to a much more livable place, which will last for one thousand years. The story ends with a big, huge, enormous surprise.

Paperback, 125 pages
5.5" x 8.5"
ISBN 1-4241-2535-9

About the author:

I am 75 years old, have a grade school education and worked twenty years for a wholesale plumbing company. I had my own business as a manufacturer's agent for plumbing materials for another twenty years, then retired at age 60. Married with four children, my wife, Marion, and I celebrated our 50th wedding anniversary on September 11, 2004—a most infamous day to have a celebration. Over the years I have invented many items, some with success, some still neither proven nor disproven. I had the enjoyment of learning how to play a tenor saxophone at age 50 with Westwood Community Band and have continued to play with the same band for twenty-five years.

Available to all bookstores nationwide.
www.publishamerica.com

Also available from PublishAmerica

SCRAP PAPER
by Brandon Hildreth

Scrap Paper is a collection of poems written by Brandon Hildreth that touch on feelings and emotions ranging from the lovely light hearted to the darkest most selfish. It is something to which everyone will be able to relate and connect during times of happiness or sadness, anger or love. It is but a few deep-seeded, subtle things that make up a life. *Scrap Paper* is what it is.

Paperback, 113 pages
5.5" x 8.5"
ISBN 1-4241-9591-8

About the author:

Brandon Hildreth currently lives in Charlotte with his two children.

Available to all bookstores nationwide.
www.publishamerica.com

Also available from PublishAmerica

FRANKIE STARGAZER'S ULTIMATE BATTLE

by Josie A. Butler

The catastrophe was almost upon the unsuspecting planet. The evil leader and his minions were wreaking havoc on mankind's gullible consciousness. Though times were simple, there was nothing innocent about what was taking place in the minds and hearts of people. Little did they know there was a secret evil taking root. There's an appointed time for everything, a time for every event under heaven. It's time to let go of the world we know and get ready for the things to come. As the most unique super hero the world has ever known, Force Fighter Frankie Stargazer encounters the final ultimate battle. The answer to evil will elude the wicked. *Frankie Stargazer's Ultimate Battle* appeals to family situations, romance and the conflicts that take place between the forces of good and evil. The story culminates into the end of time as we know it. And the beginning of a new time.

Paperback, 164 pages
5.5" x 8.5"
ISBN 1-60672-616-1

About the author:

I'm a cancer survivor and an author of four books, two true stories, *Heart of a Victim in Harm's Way* and *Beyond the Kissing Door*, and two fiction-fantasy stories, *Awesome Adventures of Frankie Stargazer* and *Frankie Stargazer's Ultimate Battle*. I wrote several screenplays, which I hope will be produced onto the big screen someday.

Available to all bookstores nationwide.
www.publishamerica.com